SHADOWS
IN THE
BASEMENT

ALAN BROWN

This is a work of fiction. Names, characters, places, and incidents are products of the author's imagination or are used fictitiously and are not to be construed as real. Any resemblance to actual events, locations, organizations, or persons, living or dead, is entirely coincidental.

World Castle Publishing, LLC
Pensacola, Florida
Copyright © Alan Brown 2022
Paperback ISBN: 9781956788860
Paperback ISBN: 9781956788846
eBook ISBN: 9781956788853
First Edition World Castle Publishing, LLC, April 25, 2022
http://www.worldcastlepublishing.com
Licensing Notes
Cover: Karen Fuller
Editor: Maxine Bringenberg

CHAPTER 1
THE HOUSE ON THE HILL

"Detective Baczenas?"

"Yes, how can I help you?"

"I want to report a number of murders."

Will Baczenas, lead detective for the Kansas City police force, looked over the man in front of him with curiosity. He was in his mid to late twenties, with thinning light brown hair, a slender build, and sad, dark eyes. He had seen this person before, but didn't recognize him.

"Maybe you better take a seat. What's your name?"

"Kevin Collins, sir."

"Yes, I remember you."

The detective took out a note pad, grabbed a pen, and began to write.

"All right, Mr. Collins, suppose you tell me what this is all about."

"I probably should have reported him years ago. I wanted to, but I was scared of him. He's a very sick person. If he knew I was talking to you right now, he'd kill me."

"Who are you talking about?"

"My brother, Detective. His name is Dennis Collins, and he's been murdering people for over ten years."

***

Will Baczenas made an intimidating presence—6'5", nearly 250 pounds, and not a bit of it was fat. He had been a detective with the Kansas City police force for nearly twenty-two years, and had locked up over a hundred criminals over those years. But there was one criminal whose crimes had gone unsolved. There was one criminal that ate at him every day, that he thought about constantly. His crimes surfaced in his nightmares over and over again. He knew of at least five disappearances tied to that psychopath. There were likely many more. He had eluded police. But like most psychopaths, he would eventually get caught.

Although, if it wasn't for his brother, this psychopath might have continued his killing spree for many more years, the detective thought.

The bodies of his victims had never been found. Hell, there wasn't even proof they were murdered. The victims of his crimes had disappeared without a trace, never heard of again and presumed dead. Detective Baczenas had always thought they were murdered, and assumed a serial killer was responsible. But he had never been close to solving the crimes. There was never anything to tie the disappearances together. Without bodies, there was no DNA to check. The few witnesses that had come forward over the years were of little help.

He had suspected Dennis Collins in the disappearances

for nearly two years. There was only circumstantial evidence that a crime had taken place. But thanks to Kevin Collins, he might finally be able to arrest his prime suspect. With his brother's testimony, he could get a search warrant and bring Dennis Collins in.

He pulled into the long, winding, asphalt driveway leading to 411 Bahman Drive. The rain was pounding. He had his windshield wipers on high, but they were of little help. The rain was coming down in sheets. It was difficult to see more than a few feet in front of the car. He flipped the bright lights on, but the glare from lights hitting the wall of rain caused the light to shoot back at him, nearly blinding him. He dimmed the headlights as he drove up the driveway.

The house, a good hundred yards off the main street, was relatively secluded. There were no lights on, neither outside nor inside. He pulled up next to the garage and turned off the engine.

He remembered this house now. He had been there years before, twice as a matter of fact. In both cases, he was investigating a disappearance and had interviewed Dennis. Neither time did he appear suspicious. Neither time did his statements prove untrue. There was no reason to suspect him in either disappearance.

The house was a three-story colonial, old and in bad need of repair. It looked like it had been built around the turn of the century. Its paint was peeling, and the floor boards on the front porch were rotting and weathered. The house had not been taken care for a long while. It looked like it had been abandoned years ago.

Detective Baczenas stepped out of the car, pulling

his gun from his shoulder holster and holding it in his right hand. He held a flashlight in his left. The rain pelted him as he walked slowly to the front porch. Much of the wood on the porch had warped — some pieces had fallen off completely. He shined the flashlight down to illuminate the area directly in front of him. Then he walked up the stairs and onto the front porch at a gingerly pace, careful not to step on any loose or damaged boards. When he reached the front door, he rang the doorbell. There was no sound. He knocked on the door loudly. There was no response. There were no lights. He heard no movement inside. It appeared to him that no one was home.

He tried the door, knob, and to his surprise the door was unlocked. He opened the door and made his presence known.

"This is Detective Baczenas with the Kansas City Police Department. I've got a warrant for Dennis Collins. If you are here, please show yourself."

There was no response.

He came into the foyer, shutting the door behind him. The detective lifted the flashlight to shine on the walls around him. There was a light switch. He flipped it, but the light did not turn on.

The electricity has been turned off, he thought.

His flashlight provided minimal visibility. He walked a few feet, stopped, shined the flashlight in all directions around him, and satisfied that no one was around, he moved another few feet and repeated the process. The rain pounding on the roof and windows and crackles of thunder were all he could hear until he heard the sound of water dripping from an area not far in front of him. The sound was coming from the kitchen.

Maybe it's water dripping from a faucet, he thought.

But when he got to the source of the sound, he discovered it was a leak from the roof, falling from the ceiling and bouncing off the floor. There were several leaks from the ceiling in the kitchen. He discovered more in the hallway leading to the stairs.

Detective Baczenas took his time checking every room on the main level—the living room, the study, the dining room, and the kitchen. The first floor had a minimal amount of furniture, and what was there appeared old and in deteriorating condition. The house did not appear to have been lived in for some time. Cobwebs dropped from the corner of walls and from areas on the ceiling. The house was cold. Cracks in the walls and window allowed cold air from the outside to penetrate the house. It was March, a chilly month in Kansas City, unusually cold and rainy this year. If someone was living in the house, the heat should have been on.

Either the utilities were shut off or someone turned them off, he thought.

Satisfied that no one was on the main floor, the detective started to climb the winding staircase to the second floor. Some of the stair boards were loose. The railing was cracked and had completely broken off in two spots.

If the brothers lived here, they certainly never took care of the place, he thought.

Every step he took on the staircase made a squeaking noise. The steps bowed downward with the weight of his body. The handrail was weak and gave him no support. If the stairs gave way, he would tumble all the way down.

His flashlight and his ears had given him no indication that anyone was in the house, but he had a sick feeling in his gut that someone was watching him. When he reached the top of the stairs he turned around and shined the flashlight toward the first floor. He thought he saw something, but there was nothing there now.

Probably just my imagination playing tricks on me, he thought.

Detective Baczenas was rarely afraid of anything. He had served as a Green Beret in Afghanistan when he was young. He had been captured, tortured, and kept prisoner in a hole in the ground not much bigger than a coffin. He learned early in his captivity not to show fear. The Taliban fed off fear. They relished it, and it made them want to inflict more pain and cause more fear. So, he learned to contain his emotions. With time, the fear dissipated completely. He became immune to it. After eighteen-months in captivity, he managed to escape and was found by an American patrol. A week later he was sent back to the States. A month after that, he was given an honorable discharge, and a week later he applied for the police academy.

Fear was not a weakness of his. But something about that old house on the hill sent chills down his spine. He wished now that he had not come alone.

He turned the flashlight to shine on the area on the second floor. There was a bathroom straight ahead. The door was open and he had a partial view of the sink and bathtub. The curtain on the tub was closed. He moved the flashlight to his left and saw a long narrow hallway, and another to his right. He decided to search the bathroom first. When he got to the doorway, he heard the dripping sound of water coming from the faucet in the sink. He shined the flashlight toward it. There were small drips of water dropping every five seconds. He turned the handle to the left and it shut off.

The handle was not turned all the way off. It could have been running for some time, he thought to himself.

The water dripping did give him pause, though. He turned the handle all the way on. Water poured out of the faucet. He turned it off.

Funny, he thought. *The water is on but the electricity and gas heat are off. If the utility companies turned everything off, they would have surely turned the water off too.*

He made a mental note to check with the utility companies the next day.

He shined the flashlight throughout the bathroom. It was a small room, maybe a hundred square feet or so. There was nothing. But the shower curtain was closed—he could not see behind it. He shined the flashlight on the curtain, thinking that if someone was hiding behind it their shadow would show through the light. There was something, a small shadow emerging just above the upper edge of the bathtub.

Something is in there, he told himself.

"Whoever is in the bathtub, come out now," he yelled.

There was no response.

Detective Baczenas raised his gun, took a deep breath, and moved his left hand to the edge of the shower curtain. He steadied the gun and pulled the curtain back. Inside the bathtub were eight small animals—mostly birds, a squirrel, and a large racoon—all dead, and all stuffed, most likely by a taxidermist. Each looked remarkably alive. They all looked like they were attacking. They all looked afraid, like one would expect them to look when they were cornered and fighting for their lives. The animals were standing up in the bathtub, almost like they were purposely positioned there, their heads lifted just above the edge of the bathtub, causing small shadows when the light from the flashlight illuminated the outside of the curtain.

The detective took another deep breath, more of a sign of relief, and lowered his gun. His adrenaline was pumping now. His heart was pounding.

He left the bathroom and started down the hall to his right. It was a narrow hallway, maybe four feet wide, with a tall ceiling. A flowery wallpaper, light blue in color with a mixture of yellow and red flowers, adorned the walls. The wallpaper was old and fading, hanging loose in several spots and ripped from the wall in others.

The first room he came to was on his right. The door was closed. He turned the knob and slowly opened the door, pointing his flashlight toward the opening. There was a small window on the other side of the room. Its curtain was ragged, and one side had fallen off completely. The rain was pounding on the window, and some moisture was coming through a crack that ran down one side of the window. The moisture had built up on the inside, causing a sort of fog and making it impossible to see outside. A flash of lightning glowed through the window, and was followed by a clap of thunder.

He shined the flashlight around the room. There were posters on the wall—one of Eric Clapton, one of Lobo, one of Farrah Fawcett in a bikini. The posters were worn, old, and faded. On another wall was a banner from Belton High School. Two bowling trophies sat on a nightstand next to the bed. The trophies were covered in dust, the plaque attached to the base of the trophy faded and difficult to read.

"Dennis Collins, 1999 League High Average," it said.

The trophy was nearly ten-years old.

The room did not look like it had been used for many years. But there was one unusual thing about it. The bed looked like it had been freshly made. The covers were clean and smelled fresh. When the detective pulled the cover back, the sheets underneath were clean. The bed sheets and cover looked like they had been recently changed.

This is Dennis's bedroom, he thought.

Other than the bed, a standard size, and the night stand, there was no other furniture in the room. On the other side of the room was a closet, its door closed.

Detective Baczenas moved to it, lifted his gun with one hand, and pointed the flashlight toward it with his other. He turned the knob and slowly opened the door.

At nearly the same moment he opened the door a flash of lightning shot across the room, followed by a loud bang. A lightning bolt either hit the house or landed nearby. The crack of it rocked the house, and a shelf fell from the back of the closet wall. The shelf caught the detective on the forehead and left shoulder, knocking the flashlight out of his hand. He fell to the floor, and the shelf and its contents fell on top of him.

He felt the fur and bone land on top of him, along with the shelf. He struggled to free himself. The weight of the shelf was pushing on his chest. It had buried his left arm underneath the debris. He couldn't see a thing, although he felt the objects rubbing against him. One was on his face. He was still holding the gun in his right hand. He moved the hand toward his face in an effort to move the objects off him, but they were buried between him and the shelf. His right leg was free. He used it to push the shelf far enough so he could pull his body out from underneath. Once free, he placed his hands on the floor, moving them backward, sideward, and frontward to locate the flashlight.

The light from it had turned off when it hit the floor. He hoped it wasn't broken. That was the only flashlight he had with him.

A couple of minutes later his left hand felt the edge of the flashlight. He grabbed hold of it, stood up, and took another deep breath before turning it on.

The light flickered once, twice, and finally turned on. He was relieved.

He turned the flashlight to the closet where the shelf lay on the floor, its contents scattered. The objects on the shelf were more animals, dead and stuffed just like the others in the bathtub.

There were three shirts and two pairs of jeans hanging up in the closet, nothing else.

Down that hallway were two more rooms, both filled with more dead animals, more products of a taxidermist. There was no furniture in either room, only rows and rows of dead animals stuffed and looking like they were ready to attack. The rows of animals on the floors of both rooms were neatly organized, all lined in perfect rows, with walking space between each row. Animals were placed in rows with similar kinds. One room had all birds—blue jays in one row, black birds in another and so on. The other room had all smaller four-legged creatures — squirrels in one row, raccoons in another, beavers in another.

Detective Baczenas turned his attention to the hallway on the other side of the bathroom. He moved slowly down the hall, focusing his flashlight on the floor ahead of him. The hallway widened just before the bathroom, and opened to a large space between the bathroom and the stairs. There was a painting on the wall overlooking the stairway he had not noticed before. It was the picture of a family — husband, wife, and a newborn baby. The picture was a black and white photo, and was absent of dust and cobwebs, as if it had been recently dusted.

The hallway on the other side of the bathroom was identical to the other hallway. On the right was one room. Its door was open — the only one of the rooms that had its door open. He beamed the flashlight inside. It was filled with clothes, women's clothes, all of a style that was reminiscent of ten or fifteen-years ago. The clothes were dusty and smelled of mothballs. But all were hung carefully on wooden hangers, organized by color and by type. Several rows of shoes hung below a bench in the middle of the room. A large, long mirror hung from the ceiling to the floor on one side. The detective moved the flashlight around the room, brushing clothes to the side to see if anything was hidden behind them. He found nothing.

Directly across the hall was another room, the only other one on the second floor.

He opened the door slowly, pointing the flashlight inside the room as he did. It was a large bedroom. There were two dressers, a large bed with a canopy, and two nightstands, one on either side. There was also a changing table with a large mirror. On the near side of the room was another door. He opened it. Inside was a bathroom with two sinks, a toilet, a large oval bathtub, and a shower with a glazed glass door. There was no one in the bathroom.

He turned and shined the flashlight on the bed at the other side of the room. The covers were lifted—it looked like someone or something was underneath them. The lump underneath the covers became more obvious the closer he got to the bed. The lump was on the right side of the bed near the edge. He moved to the opposite side of the bed, studying the object, looking for any movement, listening for any sound of life. There was none.

He took a deep breath, steadied his gun with his right hand and shining the flashlight on the bed with his left. He laid the flashlight down on the bed to free his left hand. Then he leaned over the bed, and with one quick movement of that hand he pulled the covers off.

What he saw caused him to stagger backwards and hit the corner of the nightstand. In the bed, underneath the cover, was the embalmed body of a woman in her late thirties or early forties. Heavy make-up had been applied to the corpse, while her hair, long and flowing down her back, looked like she had just stepped out of a beauty parlor. Her nails were long, manicured, and freshly painted. Her bright blue eyes, which sported blue eyeliner and long, dark lashes, were wide open. She was dressed in a bright red cocktail dress, with spaghetti straps and a low neckline that complimented her large boobs. The dress was short, barely covering her ass. Her legs were long and tanned. She wore six-inch red, high-heeled shoes. The woman looked like she was preparing to party.

That's when he heard the sound of someone running downstairs. He rushed out of the room and down the stairs. He shined the flashlight toward the main level. He saw a shadow, a large shadow, moving quickly through the downstairs foyer and toward the kitchen. He followed. He was in the foyer, twenty feet from the kitchen, when he heard a door close.

He followed the sound to the kitchen. On one side of the kitchen next to the pantry was a door. He had seen it earlier but decided not to check it until after he finished looking upstairs. He pointed the gun directly at the door and opened it. There were stairs leading down to a dark basement. He shined the flashlight toward the bottom of the stairs and began to walk down them.

His left foot had just landed on the second step when he felt something crack into the back of his head. The pain didn't register at first. He staggered forward just enough to catch the edge of his heel on the corner of a step. That sent him flying forward, and he tumbled down the basement stairs.

CHAPTER 2
BROKEN MIRROR

Fifteen years earlier.

The boy lay underneath the covers on his bed with the blanket pulled tightly around his body. His heart was pounding. His breathing was heavy. His boney, twelve-year-old body was shaking. He buried his face into the pillow, hoping, praying that his father wouldn't hear him.

Dennis had hidden underneath those covers many times in the past, too many to count. He wished he could be more like his brother. Kevin wasn't afraid of his father. He wasn't afraid of anything. He bet his brother wasn't hiding under the covers.

"He wouldn't take crap from Dad," Dennis said to himself.

Kevin had been beaten too many times to count for standing up to his father. Dennis often wondered why his brother was so defiant. It made his father so angry, and he wasn't a man that you wanted to get angry. His brother wore the scars of the belt like a badge of honor.

"He thinks he can hurt me, but he can't," Kevin would say. "I'm stronger than he is, and someday he is going to find that out."

The beatings Kevin endured were much more severe than those given to Dennis. His father wanted to hear crying. His father wanted to hear him beg for the beating to stop. But Kevin wouldn't give him that satisfaction. He never cried, no matter how painful the beating was. He just laid there on the bed, emotionless and quiet. His father broke many a belt buckle trying to make him cry. Finally, from exhaustion or sometimes because his weapon of choice had failed him, his father would stop.

Kevin just laid there, bleeding and cut. A belt buckle can leave a lot of damage. A few minutes later, after his father had gone away, his mother would come in with antiseptic and bandages and relieve some of his pain.

Ron Collins was a drunk, and not a good drunk either — he was a mean drunk. Every night he came home from work, sat in his recliner, and started drinking. A fifth of bourbon and a six pack of beer, every night. Weekends and holidays were much worse. He didn't work on weekends or holidays, so that provided him another nine hours of drinking time. He would start drinking when he woke up and continue all day and night. If the family was lucky, he would pass out before the violence started. More often than not, they weren't that lucky.

The scream of his mother followed by the sound of glass breaking caused Dennis to start crying that night. He tried to muffle his cries with the pillow, but Kevin could hear them.

"Be quiet, Dennis," Kevin whispered. "You don't want him to hear you."

But Dennis couldn't stop. He had lost control of his emotions. His breathing was short, and loud. His entire body was shaking beneath the blanket, so much so that the bed began creaking, softly at first, but soon gaining in intensity. His body began rocking back and forth in the bed. Kevin had seen his brother's body rock violently in bed many times in the past when his fear took control of him. The rocking motion caused the bed to squeak. The more it squeaked, the more Dennis rocked. His fear was exacerbated by the noise he was making. Every cry, every shake of his body meant a greater chance that his father would hear him, and God help him if he did.

Dennis felt sorry for his mother. She had been on the receiving side of his father's anger many times in the past. But, if given a choice, he would rather have his father unleash his demons on his mother than on him. She, after all, married the son of a bitch. She could have left him many times, but she never did.

Kevin told him, "Mom is a fucking coward. She lets him beat her and does nothing about it. That's sick enough. But to allow him to beat us and inflict as much pain and damage on us as he can without doing something about it, is fucking insane. She deserves what she gets."

Dennis and Kevin remembered at least a dozen times when their mother packed their bags and left her husband while he was at work. Every time, she came back within a day or two. She always said that she loved him and forgave him. And for a few days after she returned to him, he would change. His drinking slowed and the beatings stopped for a while. But they would always start up again.

Kevin blamed his mother as much as he did his father for the violent attacks. Dennis, however, was sympathetic toward his mother. In his eyes, she was as much of a victim as he was. Besides, she always took time to comfort Dennis after one of his father's beatings. She loved him—he knew it. She was the only one that really did love him. Sure, Kevin stood up for him. Kevin was his protector. But he never showed empathy. Kevin was strong and independent, and Dennis felt safe when he was around. But Kevin was emotionless, incapable of showing sympathy. On the outside, he seemed innocent and harmless. But his heart was cold and callous.

Their mother's screams from the bedroom were deafening. The crash of breaking glass was followed by something hitting the wall and then a loud thump on the floor. They were sounds the brothers had heard all too often.

"Better her than us," Kevin whispered to his brother.

"We should do something, Kevin. He's going to kill her this time. I know it."

"Shut up, Dennis. He'll hear you. Besides, that bitch deserves it for putting up with his shit for so long. She could have left him. She could have protected us, but she just had to come back. Now she's paying the price for it."

"Stop him, Kevin. You can do it. I know you're not afraid of him."

"You stop him, Dennis. Oh, that's right, you're too much of a fucking coward. Just hide under your blanket like you always do and wait for it to stop. But try not to wet the bed tonight, okay."

Their mother's screams would eventually stop. They always did, sometimes because she lost consciousness, other times because their father just got tired of beating her. The worst times were when their mother passed out before their father had taken out all his anger on her. That's when he would come looking for Dennis. Dennis was his next favorite target. He didn't fight back like Kevin. He laid there and took the beating without resistance. He was just like his mother.

After the loud thump on the floor, there was silence in their parents' bedroom.

"Maybe he is done," Dennis whispered.

"We'll find out soon enough, Dennis," Kevin said.

With any luck, their father was satisfied with the beating he gave their mother and now he would go to sleep. But Dennis wasn't a lucky person. The door flew open to the boys' bedroom. Their father staggered in carrying a belt with an oversized belt buckle.

"Dammit Dennis, I can hear you. You should have been asleep hours ago."

Dennis tightened his hold on the blanket covering him in the bed. Ron Collins ripped it off the bed and flung it on the floor. Dennis laid shivering from fear, his head buried in the pillow, his heart racing.

"Take off your pajama bottoms," he told Dennis.

When Dennis didn't react fast enough, his father pulled them off him, exposing his underwear and bare legs.

"Please don't, Dad," Dennis begged.

Fear only excited his father more. He wrapped his belt

and lifted it high.

That's when Kevin pounded him over the head with his baseball bat. He never saw it coming. Their father fell quickly to the ground, blood seeping through a wound on the back of his head. He was out cold.

"Okay, let's drag him back into the bedroom. He probably won't even remember what happened to him when he wakes up in the morning," Kevin said.

"Thanks, Kevin," Dennis said.

"You're going to need to grow some balls, Dennis. I won't always be here to take care of you."

The brothers grabbed their father's feet and dragged him into the bedroom. They left him on the floor next to the bed. Their mother was laying on the other side of the floor next to broken glass. The mirror on her dresser was shattered, and there were small amounts of blood dripping from the remaining glass onto the dresser.

Dennis checked his mother — — she was breathing. He went to the bathroom and filled a cup with water, brought it back, and poured it on her face. She coughed and her eyes opened.

"Mother, are you all right?" Dennis asked.

"Yes, I think so. Help me into bed and get me three aspirin."

Dennis did as his mother asked. Kevin went back to his room, disgusted with his mother for putting up with the beatings.

"He's going to kill you one of these times," Kevin said as he walked out of the room.

After covering his mother and turning out the lights,

Dennis went back to his room. Kevin was in bed waiting for him.

"You need to clean up the blood on the floor and change your sheets. You pissed the bed again. Better change your pajamas too. They smell. Also, wash yourself up. I don't want to smell urine all night."

"I will, Kevin."

"Dennis, you know he's going to kill her one of these nights."

"I know."

"Dennis, it doesn't need to happen."

"What do you mean?"

"We can stop it. We can stop him."

"No, Kevin, we can't do that."

"Not we, Dennis. You need to do it. He won't expect it coming from you."

"No, Kevin. You're crazy. I could never hurt anyone."

"I know. That's why he would never expect you to try to hurt him. But if you're too afraid, you can just wait for him to kill our mother and then come after you."

***

Ron Collins didn't remember anything that occurred that night when he woke up the next day. His head pounded and he had a large bump on the back of his head. He assumed his headache was the result of too much drinking. He assumed the bump on his head was the result of falling out of bed. He had done that many times before.

He had often blacked out when he really tied one on, so it wasn't unusual that he had no memory of the previous night's events. But he knew that dark side had showed up the night before when he saw the shattered mirror and the facial bruises on his wife.

"I'm so sorry, honey," he told his wife.

Jane Collins had heard those words so many times before. She knew her husband meant it, but she also knew it would happen again.

"You really hurt me this time, Ron. I think I need to go to the hospital."

"No, you'll be fine. I can't take you to the hospital. You know that, Jane. Take some aspirin and a hot bath. You'll feel a lot better. I'll make you some breakfast and a cup of coffee."

"Ron, you can't keep doing this to me. I think you may have broken a rib this time."

"I'm sorry. You know I love you. It won't happen again."

It would happen again. His wife knew that. She feared her husband when he drank. He became a different person, a monster. She knew he would hurt her again, maybe worse next time. But she loved her husband too much to leave him. She had tried before, several times, but she always went back. Part of her said he loved her and she loved him. Part of her was afraid of what he would do to her if she didn't go back to him.

Ron helped his wife out of bed and walked her into the bathroom. He started the bath water and left to go into the kitchen and make her some breakfast.

Jane was so sore. Every muscle in her body ached. It was a struggle to take her nightgown off. After it was off, she examined her body to assess the damage. Large, dark purple bruises were on her shoulder, arm, and stomach. Her back hurt like hell. She moved to the mirror to see the damage he had done to her face. Her left cheek was swollen and bruised, her forehead had a long cut where the blood had caked, and her left eye was blackened. She took a wash cloth, dampened it, and gently rubbed the dried blood on her forehead. When the dried blood was removed, it revealed a cut about two inches long.

She couldn't see the damage to her back, but from the soreness she thought there must be a lot of bruising. She lifted a vanity mirror and held it up behind her back. The reflection in the mirror showed two large bruises on her upper back and one on her lower back.

"At least there's nothing that will leave a permanent mark," she said quietly to herself.

Jane Collins was a child bride—she'd married three days after her fourteenth birthday, three months pregnant. She had met Ron Collins at Al's Drive-in, a local hamburger and malt diner that was popular with the teenage crowd. Ron had just served a three-year stint in the marines, and had been discharged a month earlier. He was ten-years her senior, and miles ahead of her in experience. He had been married once to a high school sweetheart. He married her not long after he was drafted and just before he was shipped off to Viet Nam. The war changed him—or maybe it just brought out a dark side in him that had been buried for so long. When he came home on leave a year into their marriage, he was a bitter, angry person that took comfort in the bottle. He beat the hell out of his wife. She left him and never returned. He learned of his divorce in a letter while he was stationed overseas.

In Ron, Jane saw a strong man, much like her father.

He was handsome, kind, and generous, and he was her first love. Three months after they started dating, she became pregnant. In those days, growing up in a strict, God-fearing family, there wasn't much choice. She would need to marry Ron to make it right in the eyes of the Lord and her family. She never saw his dark side while they were dating. He didn't let that evil come out until after they were married.

They bought an old, four-bedroom, two story house with a large wooden porch to start their life together. The house, set two-miles outside the city of Belton and twenty-miles south of Kansas City, was an old, abandoned farmhouse that sat on five acres of land. No one had lived in it for years. The roof leaked, windows were broken, and the wood exterior was warping and in bad need of paint. The porch was worn and in poor condition. Ron got a great price for it, and since he was handy with repairs, he figured he could get the house in good condition in no time.

From the accounts his mother shared with him, Dennis believed the early part of their marriage was very happy. His father had a good job at the Ford Plant in Kansas City. He spent his spare time working on the house. He repaired the rooms, re-painted the exterior and interior of the house, and re-enforced and painted the front porch. He even helped his wife design and furnish a nursery.

When they learned that Jane was pregnant with twin boys both were ecstatic, although a little concerned about money. The home repairs had drained their savings. The unexpected expense of twins was both a blessing and a cause for anxiety.

A few months before her due date, Jane began

experiencing some health problems. She needed bed rest. That and the increasing doctor bills increased Ron's stress level substantially. That's when he began drinking more heavily. The drinking numbed him. It helped him relax and forget about his troubles for a little while.

The beatings started the night they learned Jane was going to have twin boys. Ron had been fine with the news earlier that day, but concerns about money and the added responsibility of raising two boys caused him to drink. The drinking caused him to blame Jane for their financial situation. The more he drank, the angrier he got. He had never hit Jane before, but that changed late that night. It wasn't anything in particular that set him off. Jane came in the living room to tell her husband she was tired and was going to bed. She gave him a kiss on the cheek. He pushed her away. She said something about it and he slapped her, hard enough to send her backwards and cause her to lose her balance and fall to the ground. He apologized to her for two days. But the physical violence got worse from that day on.

Jane's parents tried to convince her to leave him, but she was determined to stay. After every beating, he told her how sorry he was and how it would never happen again. But that was a promise he never kept. When he sobered up the next day after a beating, he was so remorseful. For a while, she clung to hope that he would stop drinking and stop beating her. She was wrong.

The birth of her twins was difficult. She had some internal bleeding from a beating her husband had given her the day before she went into labor. A "C" section had to be performed. For a while the doctors weren't sure if either the babies or Jane would survive. They did, but not without damage. The doctors didn't know if Jane would be able to bear any more children. Dennis had brain damage.

"You're slow because of what our father did to our mother," Kevin would often say.

For a while after the birth of the twins, Ron gave up drinking. He even started going to AA meetings. He was remorseful about the beating he'd given Jane, the one that sent her into premature labor, the one that was, at least partly, responsible for the boys' problems.

For over six months he was sober. He took up a taxidermy hobby, something his father had done when he was young. He fixed up the basement, bought the chemicals and supplies he needed, and began spending his free time in the basement. The hobby helped take his mind off drinking. It worked for a while.

But the death of his parents in an automobile accident a few months later sent his life spiraling out of control again. He went back to the bottle and never attended another AA meeting.

Jane never talked to anyone about the beatings her husband gave her. Part of her was ashamed, and the other part was afraid of what her husband would do if she did tell anyone. She used make-up to cover the bruises, and clothing to cover the bruises that make-up couldn't hide. Her parents suspected what was happening. They tried to convince her to leave him, but she always denied that he was hurting her and refused to leave him.

There were times she ran from him, but she never went to her parents. She would usually spend the night in a car, usually in the park. Dennis and Kevin remembered many nights they'd spent in the back seat of the family car listening to their mother cry. She always went back to him the next morning. He always apologized for what he had done, even though, in most cases, he had no recollection of the events. For a few days things would be good, and then the cycle would start over again.

When the bathtub was full, Jane got in. The water burned as it soaked the cuts on her body. Her dry blood dampened and colored the water an ugly shade of pink. She gently wiped her wounds and waited for the pain to subside.

A few minutes later, Ron appeared in the bathroom with a plate of scrambled eggs and fried Spam, and a hot cup of black coffee. Post-beatings were about the only time her husband cooked anything. He would pamper her for a day or two while her wounds healed, as if a couple of days of tenderness would make up for the horror of what he had done. Jane knew her husband loved her, and regretted what he had done. But she also knew his first love would always be the bottle, and when the call of that first love became too great, he would return to it and the beatings would start all over again.

"He can't help himself. It is a disease," she told herself.

Kevin and Dennis would fend for themselves during their mother's healing period. They would make their own food, go to school, and stay out of the house as much as possible until their mother was able to care for them again. This was normally a safe period for the brothers. Their father was on his best behavior while their mother healed. But that wasn't to say they could be normal children. They had to be quiet and avoid their father as much as possible. Even if he didn't beat them then for misbehaving now, he most likely would later. They made their own food, did their household chores, went to school, and remained quiet when they were home. They avoided their father as much as they could. The brothers learned to whisper inside the house, never raising their voices. If they felt the need to talk or make noise, they went outside and away from the house. They constantly walked on eggshells around their father. But that was slowly changing for one of the brothers.

While Dennis reverted into a shell, afraid to give his father any reason to give him a beating, Kevin was becoming less and less afraid of their father. Dennis became introverted. He had always been on the shy side, but when he was home, he rarely talked for fear of saying something that might set his father off. His body cowered under the covers at night. It shook beneath the bed sheets, at times rocking slowly back and forth to settle his fear. His bed wetting became a nightly occurrence. Their mother hid it from their father. She came in the boys' bedroom every morning, changed the sheets, and threw Dennis's clothes and bed sheets into the laundry. She never said a word about it. Dennis would clean himself in the bathroom before coming to the breakfast table.

Jane had a special love for Dennis, perhaps because he was born with challenges, perhaps because he needed her much more than Kevin. Kevin had always been strong. He was a survivor. He didn't need his mother's help.

The bruises on Jane's body healed in a few days and Ron went back to drinking. Every night he sat in his recliner, parked in front of the television set in the living room. Next to him, on a table, was a bottle of Old Crow and a shot glass. In his right hand was a cold can of beer, usually Pabst, but anything cheap was fine with him.

"They all taste the same after the first three," he used to say.

He would fill his shot glass with Old Crow and down it in one quick gulp. Then he would chase it down with a can of cold beer, one after another after another.

"Jane, grab me another beer," was repeated about every twenty minutes throughout the night.

Jane normally stayed in the kitchen, avoiding her husband, except to bring him a fresh beer—waiting, always waiting for the violence to begin. Some nights, good nights, he passed out before his dark side could take over. But there was always that constant fear that something would trigger his rage before he passed out. Those were the nights that petrified Jane and Dennis.

On a stormy night a few weeks later, Ron came home early from work. He had been fired again. He was in a mean mood when he walked through the door that evening, his breath reeking of cheap beer and whiskey. Jane had seen this before. He was pissed at the world. He'd stopped by a tavern on the way home, drank until he either got thrown out of the bar or cut off from the bartender, and was forced to come home to continue his drinking. Jane knew how this night would end. She sent Dennis and Kevin to their room and made them promise not to come out. Her only hope was that he would pass out before he got violent, but she knew there was little chance at that. He was too restless, too upset to relax enough to pass out. She knew what was going to happen that night.

***

As the storm intensified outside, so did the storm brewing in her husband's head. Dennis and Kevin laid in bed, silently listening to the thunder and lightning outside. Dennis tried to concentrate on the howling wind and rain pounding against their bedroom window. He knew what was coming too.

The noise outside was loud, but not loud enough to cover up their father's anger. It was only a matter of time before his yelling would turn into action. Jane begged her husband not to hit her, but she may as well have been talking to the wall. Ron was not listening. His dark side had taken control. Her first screams made Dennis jump. The loud crash on the wall followed by the shaking of the floor caused Dennis to unload his bladder on the bed. He began rocking back and forth as he clutched the bed covers tightly around his body.

"This is it, bro," Kevin said softly. "He's going to kill her tonight."

"Shut up, Kevin," Dennis whispered, his voice cracking.

"You want me to stop him?" Kevin asked.

"How are you going to stop him?" Dennis asked.

"It's better that you don't know, Dennis. Because if I do, I don't want you ratting on me."

"I wouldn't do that."

"Dennis, you're a fucking pussy. You know you would tell on me at the first sign of trouble."

Outside their bedroom door, the two brothers could hear their mother's cries. Then they heard her body being dragged through the hallway into their parents' bedroom. Ron Collins slammed the bedroom door behind them. That's where the most violent attacks on their mother would take place.

"Please, Kevin. You've got to stop him. I promise I won't tell anyone. But you're the only one that can protect her now. Please just stop him," Dennis begged his brother.

Kevin picked up a baseball bat from under his bed, got up, and walked out of the bedroom, shutting the door behind him. Dennis listened as his brother walked to his parents' bedroom. The door would be locked—it was always locked when their father wanted to dish out a beating on their mother. He heard the loud knocks on his parents' door.

"Stop beating up my mother, you son of a bitch. If you need to beat up someone, why don't you try me, you fucking coward?"

Dennis had never heard his brother speak like that to their father.

He's crazy, Dennis thought. *Father is going to kill him.*

For a few seconds there was complete silence, except for the muffled cries of their mother. Then Dennis could hear his father yell, "I'm going to kick your fucking ass, boy."

Dennis heard the door to his parents' room open.

"What the hell are you running for, boy? You started this fight, now I'm going to finish it. Come back and face me, you little shit."

Dennis heard his brother running down the hallway into the kitchen. He heard his father staggering out of the bedroom and running after him.

***

"No, Ron. He didn't mean it. Please don't hurt him," he heard his mother beg.

But Ron had lost control of himself. The evil inside him was making all his decisions now. He moved quickly down the hallway, his body under the influence of too much booze, bouncing from one side of the wall to the other as he staggered through the hall.

When he got to the kitchen, his son was not there. The door leading down to the basement was open. The lights in the basement were off.

"Come on, you little shit, show yourself. It's time for you to learn a lesson. If I need to come looking for you, it's only going to hurt more."

Ron Collins grabbed a steak knife from the kitchen drawer and started down the stairs.

He sensed something was wrong an instant before he felt the baseball bat crack into his back. Ron fell hard down the stairs, his head contacting the stairs midway down. His body flipped over three times on the way.

He didn't suffer long. His neck was broken in the fall.

CHAPTER 3
A SHATTERED LIFE

Ten years after father's death

Dennis woke up in a cold sweat. The memories of his father visited him in his nightmares nearly every night. Ten years since his father fell down those stirs, and he still couldn't shake the ghosts in his past. The scars of his childhood had created open wounds in his adult life. He was alone, never been married, hadn't even had a serious relationship. He liked women — he often fantasized about them. But his social skills were non-existent. His personality was hidden inside him, deep below the scars of his past. There were only two people in the world that cared about him — his mother and Kevin.

Dennis lived in the same house he had grown up in. His mother, fragile and in poor health, lived with him. Kevin lived a few miles away. His brother had managed to live a somewhat normal life. He had escaped the home the day after his eighteenth birthday. He was always the stronger of the two. Kevin was married and had two step-daughters.

Dennis couldn't help but be a little jealous of his brother. He had a nice house, an attractive wife, and a decent job. Kevin was the type of person Dennis wanted to be. But he couldn't. He wasn't strong like his brother.

Still, life for him wasn't terrible. He was comfortable. His mother received social security, and there were still some proceeds coming in from investments their mother had made with their father's life insurance policy. They lived a frugal but comfortable life.

He took care of his mother. He cooked, cleaned, and ran errands for her. He took her to doctor's appointments and shopping. Jane suffered from depression. Most days she didn't get out of bed. Dennis brought her food, sat next to her bed, and talked to her for hours at a time. He tried to get her to smile, but smiles had been few and far between since her husband died. On good days, she sat in the living room next to Dennis and watched television or just watched people go by outside. Every time she went into a deep depression, Dennis wondered if she would ever come out of it. Eventually she would, but those periods of normality were short and far between.

He loved his mother. She had been there for him when he was younger, and he didn't mind being there for her when she needed him. But there were times, particularly lately, as her mind and body began slipping away, that he wished his brother was there to help.

Kevin had abandoned their mother when he turned eighteen. He didn't want anything to do with her. Kevin blamed her for everything that had happened when he was young. "She is weak. She can't even protect herself, let alone protect us," he used to tell Dennis. "She deserves whatever happens to her."

Kevin was immune to emotions when it came to his mother. He had survived quite well without her help, and he wasn't about to let her sad life interfere with his now.

Dennis never tried to change his brother's mind about their mother. He knew it was useless. Besides, he was comfortable with the situation staying as it was. Without his brother's involvement, his mother was completely dependent on Dennis, and he liked it that way. It made him feel needed. And his relationship with his brother had strengthened over the years. Kevin would never admit it, but Dennis knew his brother loved him and needed him. They could count on each other.

Dennis only wished Kevin's wife felt the same way toward him. She despised Dennis. That's what Kevin told him.

"She thinks you're weak and needy, like our mother. She laughs at you behind your back," he told Dennis.

Dennis had only met Marsha once. He was hurt that she would judge him that way after only one meeting.

"She's jealous of our bond," Kevin would say.

Kevin didn't want to cause problems with Marsha. Their marriage had always been on shifting ground. She was not happy with Kevin. Her love for him had dissipated, if it ever existed in the first place. She used him. He had a good job, and provided for her and her two daughters from a previous marriage. She enjoyed the life he provided for her.

She particularly enjoyed the fact that he didn't interfere with her lifestyle. Marsha liked to party. She liked men. She had never been faithful to Kevin. He wasn't the jealous type, and he never confronted her about her late nights at the bars.

"I'm partying with my girlfriends," she would tell him.

If Kevin has a weakness, it is Marsha, Dennis thought.

Kevin had always been strong. He had always remained emotionally unattached. He had never shown empathy for anyone or anything. Dennis couldn't think of even one time his brother was afraid. But there was something about Marsha that brought out his vulnerabilities. He was not strong around her. She was the dominant partner in their marriage. She controlled him and he, for some unknown reason, refused to stand up to her.

He was determined to make his marriage work, so he appeased his wife. He didn't ask questions about her late nights out. He didn't complain about her lack of affection. He didn't even get upset when she asked him to move to the spare bedroom.

"My snoring was disturbing her," he told Dennis.

And when she told him that she didn't want his brother coming around, he told Dennis to stay away. They would meet someplace else, usually a park or a bar. Kevin always called when he wanted to visit his brother.

It was a few minutes past midnight when the phone rang.

"Dennis, I need to meet with you now," his brother said.

"What? Okay. Where?" Dennis said, trying to wake from a sound sleep.

"Fuck you, bro. Where do we always meet when it's this goddamn late?"

"Okay, see you there, Kevin. Give me fifteen minutes."

"Make it ten, I'm already three beers ahead of you."

Dennis hung up the phone, walked down the hall to his mother's bedroom, and opened the door slowly to see if the phone call had awakened her. She was sound asleep. He went to his room, got dressed, and left the house. He started the engine on his twelve-year old Ford Taurus. It made a hell of a racket when it first turned over. The car had over two-hundred-thousand miles on it. It had the original engine and most of the original parts. It should have probably gone to the salvage yard years earlier, but the damn thing just kept going. Although nowadays, the sound the engine made was reminiscent of a drowning man gasping for his final breath.

Ten minutes later, Dennis pulled in the parking lot of Kelly's bar, a seedy place just off the interstate where hookers and strippers sold their services to the customers inside. Truck drivers and unhappily married men looking for adventure made up most of the clientele.

Kevin was seated at a table in a dark corner of the bar.

"Bout time you got here, bro. What the hell took you so long? I'm on my fifth beer," Kevin said.

"What's up, Kevin? Why did we need to meet so late?"

"Geez, sorry bro. I forgot it's past your bedtime. Just relax and have a drink or two."

"Waitress, bring us two more drafts."

"You ever feel like killing someone, Dennis? Maybe our poor, sick mother? Hell, you'd be doing her a favor. You'd put her out of her misery."

"No, Kevin. I've never thought of killing anyone, and certainly not our mother. What kind of sick question is that?"

"Hey, calm down, bro. It was only a question. I was just curious if you had ever thought of killing someone, 'cause I've thought about it a lot. There are a hell of lot of people out there that deserve to be killed. The world would be a better place without them."

"You're talking crazy, Kevin. I hope it's just the beer talking."

"Come on, Dennis. Aren't you curious about what it would feel like to choke the life out of someone, to watch their eyes bulge with terror, to hear them begging for their life as they gasp their last breath?"

"No, I haven't, and I hope to hell you're not serious."

"Oh, but I am, little bro. I want to know what it feels like."

"Kevin, I think I need to leave. You're acting crazy. You're frightening me."

"Settle down, have another beer. I'm just playing with you, Dennis."

Dennis couldn't help but wonder if Kevin was serious. His words told him he wasn't, but his eyes told him he was. He hadn't seen dark eyes like that since his father during one of his rages. There were many times over the years that Kevin had reminded him of his father. Like his father, Kevin was easily angered. Like his father, he drank too much, and the booze altered his behavior for the worse. There were times—this was one of them—when he was afraid of his brother.

Dennis wanted to leave. His common sense told him to stand up and walk out. His common sense told him that nothing good was going to come from this night. But he couldn't leave. Kevin wouldn't let him. He controlled Dennis—he had always controlled him. Kevin was the strong brother. Dennis was the weak one. Whatever Kevin told him to do, Dennis would do it. He was powerless to make his own decisions when Kevin was present.

"Waitress, grab us two more drafts and two shots of Old Crow," Kevin ordered.

Dennis rarely drank. His body had not built up a tolerance to alcohol. He only drank when he was with Kevin, and only because his brother insisted. It wouldn't be long before the memories of that night were completely wiped away in a drunken stupor.

The alarm clock was ringing in his ear. The morning sun was pouring through the window. His head was pounding. He laid there staring at the ceiling. The ceiling fan was on high, making a loud, squeaking noise as the fan blades swirled around at a rapid speed. He rolled over far enough to shut the alarm clock off. It took a few seconds to register that he was in his own bed. He remembered going to the bar the night before. He remembered drinking until he was dizzy. But he had no recollection of how he got home. His clothes were damp. He felt the wetness soaking through his pants and onto his bare leg underneath.

Then he noticed the red-soaked bed sheets. The red substance was on the bed sheets below him and had soaked the sheets to the very edge, gathering into a small pool at the edge of the bed and dripping small droplets onto the carpet below. He lifted his head in an effort to determine the source of the red liquid. He jumped out of bed when he realized the red substance coated his pants and much of his shirt. It was blood.

He removed his clothes, thinking the blood must be his. He had no cuts or wounds.

"Shit," he said out loud. "What happened last night?"

Then he noticed the time, 10 a.m. *Mother must be starving,* he thought.

He always made breakfast for her around seven. She would be upset that he was late with her breakfast. He wrapped up his bloody clothes and put them in a large, plastic bag. Then he put on fresh clothes and took the bag of bloodied clothes to the garage and placed them inside the trash can.

Dennis hurried into the kitchen, got out the eggs and bacon, turned on the stove, and placed two frying pans on the burners. In one he placed two strips of bacon. The other he coated with butter, then cracked two eggs and dropped them carefully into the hot skillet, careful not to break the yolks. Mother liked her eggs sunny side up, and she liked her bacon crisp with a sprinkle of brown sugar.

When done, he plated the meal, including a piece a wheat toast buttered on one side with strawberry jam. He placed the plate, silverware, a cup of black coffee, and a small glass of orange juice on a tray and took it into his mother's room.

"Where have you been, Dennis?" she asked. "I thought you forgot about me."

"I would never do that, Mother. I'm sorry. I overslept."

He left the tray on his mother's lap and went into the bathroom to shower and change. Normally Dennis would have made himself a plate of food too and sat with his mother while both ate. But he had no appetite that morning. His stomach was churning, and his head was pounding. He figured three aspirin, a hot shower, shave, and a cup of hot black coffee would make him feel a lot better.

He'd just stepped out of the shower when the doorbell rang. Dennis dried himself, put on a robe, and went to the front door.

Two men dressed in suits were at the door.

"Dennis Collins?" one of the men asked.

"Yes," Dennis replied.

Both men pulled out police badges.

"I'm Detective Baczenas and this is Detective Moffit. We'd like to ask you a few questions. Do you mind if we come in?"

Dennis hesitated for a few moments. He didn't want to let them in, but he knew they would be suspicious if he didn't. He suspected they were there about whatever happened last night. Trouble was, he had no idea what happened.

"Sure, come on in. But please be quiet. My mother is in the bedroom. She not feeling well. Can we go in the kitchen to talk? I was just about to pour myself a cup of coffee. Can I get you gentlemen a cup?"

"No thanks, we're fine, but go ahead and help yourself. You look like you might have had a rough night, Mr. Collins."

"No, just had a little trouble sleeping."

Dennis poured a cup of coffee and sat at the breakfast table. The two detectives took chairs at the table also.

"Mr. Collins, do you mind telling us where you were last night?" Detective Baczenas asked.

"I was at Kelly's Bar until late."

"How late?"

"I don't really remember, Detective. I must have drunk too much. My memory is a little foggy."

"Mr. Collins, do you remember paying for a private room for you and a lady by the name of Barbara? You may remember her by her stage name, Candy."

"No, I don't remember that. But it couldn't have been me. I've never done anything like that before. I *wouldn't* do anything like that, Detective."

"Well, someone using your credit card paid for a room at nearly three last night. The desk clerk remembers seeing a young man, about your age and build, in the company of the woman. You say your memory is foggy last night. Is it possible you don't remember paying for the room?"

"No, Detective. I'm sure I would remember doing something like that. I'm not that kind of person. I would never take a stranger back to a room. Detective, did something happen to the woman?"

"We don't know yet. The desk clerk heard a struggle coming from the room. When no one came out for a long while, he called the police. The police found evidence of violence in that room, but nobody was in it. The young woman didn't report back to work."

"Well, I can assure you, Detectives, I wasn't in that room."

"Okay, Mr. Collins. One other question, please. Do you have a recent picture of yourself?"

"Yes."

"May we have it? I assure you we will not damage it, and we'll return it as soon as possible."

"Why do you need a picture of me?"

"So we can rule you out as a suspect, if in fact, anything did happen to Barbara Johnson. You say you weren't the person that rented the room last night. We might be able to clear that up with your picture."

Dennis walked into the living room, removed a picture of himself from a photo album, and handed it to Detective Baczenas. "That photo is about two years old. That's the most recent one I have, but you can see I haven't changed much."

The detective thanked Mr. Collins and walked out the front door.

Dennis was shaking. His nerves were a wreck. He poured another cup of coffee, sat at the kitchen table, and called his brother.

"Kevin?"

"Oh, shit, bro. I just fuckn' got to bed. What the hell do you want?"

"Kevin, I just had two detectives come to my house."

"No, shit. What did you do, little bro?"

"They wanted to know about last night. They said someone used my credit card and paid for a room for one of those hookers at Kelly's."

"That was you, Dennis. You were pretty shit-faced last night."

"You know damn well it wasn't me that rented that room. It was you, Kevin."

"Careful, little bro. Did you forget who you're talking to? I'll kick your ass if you're not careful."

"It had to be you, Kevin. You got me drunk. I passed out, and you picked up one of those hookers using my credit card."

"Listen to me, Dennis, and listen carefully. I didn't pick up a hooker last night, and I didn't use your credit card. You were the one that paid for that hooker. You were the one that took her to the room, and if anything happened to that girl, you were the one that did it."

"No, that's not possible. I wouldn't do that."

"Oh, trust me, bro, you did. You were just so shit-faced you don't remember. Tell me, Dennis, what do you remember from last night?"

"I remember you called me and asked me to meet you at Kelly's. I remember going there and sitting with you. I remember having several beers, and then you started ordering shots. That's when my mind went blank. I don't remember anything after that."

"Well, let me fill in some of the blanks for you, bro. You drank more than I've ever seen you drink before. You were in complete party animal mode. I'd never seen you like that before. Do you remember the lap dances?"

"No."

"Dad would have been proud of you, Dennis. For a while last night, I thought you'd fallen in love. That girl, I think her name was Candy, was hot stuff. God, she was grinding on you like nothing I'd seen before. I told you that you needed to get a room, and that's exactly what you did. God, I can't imagine what your credit card bill must have been last night."

"No, that can't be. I've never done anything like that before."

"Bro, trust me, with enough booze in you and by choosing the wrong head to make your decisions, a person is capable of doing almost anything."

"Okay, so tell me what happened after I took her to the room?"

"Hell, Dennis, I don't know. I waited for you in the bar for a long time. When you didn't show up, I went home."

"What about the girl? Did she come back to the bar?"

"I don't know. I was pretty shit-faced myself. I don't remember seeing her, but she might have come back. Dennis, I'm only going to ask you once. You know that I won't judge you one way or another. Did you hurt that girl?"

"No, I couldn't hurt anyone. You know me, Kevin."

"Yeah, and until last night I would have sworn you couldn't hurt a fly. But last night you were a different person. I saw a side of you that even I was envious of. You were a fucking animal last night, Dennis, and you can't even remember it. You know, last night wasn't the first time you've blacked out. Remember the night our father died? You have no memory of most of that night. If I were you, bro, I'd see a good psychiatrist. Maybe they can find out what is causing your blackouts. Or are you afraid they might lock you up in some looney bin?"

Dennis hung up the phone, poured another cup of coffee, and sat silently at the table thinking about the phone call with his brother. Kevin was not one for providing empathy. He spoke his mind regardless of what other's thought.

Damn, I wish I could remember last night, Dennis thought.

He didn't want to believe it, but his gut was telling him he had done something very bad last night. His gut was also telling him he hadn't seen the last of Detective Baczenas.

His thoughts were interrupted by the sound of his

mother. Dennis hurried to her room.

"What do you need, Mother?" he asked.

"I need my pain medicine. The bottle on the nightstand is empty."

"Okay, I'll get it for you."

A minute later he came out of the bathroom with another bottle of pain medication and a glass of water. He removed two pills from the bottle and sat the remainder of the bottle on the nightstand next to his mother's bed. He handed the two pills and glass of water to his mother and turned to remove her breakfast tray. It didn't look like her food had been touched. The eggs, bacon, and toast were still there. The coffee cup was full and the coffee cool to the touch. Her juice glass was full.

"Mother, you need to eat something," he told her. "How are you ever going to get stronger if you don't eat?"

Dennis pulled the covers back over his mother, turned on the television, and carried the tray out of her room. He set the food tray down by the sink and stared at it for a few seconds.

His stomach was calmer now. His appetite was coming back. Besides, he hated to waste food. That was a habit his father had forced on him.

"Never leave the table until all the food on your plate is gone," he used to say.

Dennis picked up his mother's breakfast plate, took it over to the table, and began eating it. The food was cold now, but the flavor was still there.

Not a bad cook, Dennis said to himself. *That's one thing I learned from Mother.*

CHAPTER 4
AFTER FATHER'S DEATH

The early years after father's death

The ambulance arrived at the house fifteen minutes after the fall. There was nothing they could do. Ron Collins died of a broken neck. His lifeless body lay at the bottom of the basement stairs. Jane Collins was devastated. Dennis tried to console his mother, but it was no use. She had lost her soul mate, the only man she had ever loved. At least that was what she told everyone, including the police that investigated his death.

"I loved him with all my heart," Jane told the police. "He drank too much, but he loved me. He was a good man."

The police didn't go into their bedroom. They didn't interview the boys. If they had done either, they would have had a true picture of the relationship between Ron Collins and his wife.

When Ron Collins's blood alcohol level came back,

the medical examiner ruled the death accidental. There was no evidence of foul play, and it was quite plausible that he lost his balance and fell down the basement stairs due to his drunken state.

A funeral was arranged, and Ron's body was buried in a grave next to a waterfall in Evergreen Cemetery five days later. Other than the immediate family, only one of his three sisters attended the funeral and burial.

"Father wasn't the type of person to make friends," Kevin said.

A week later, Jane's mourning period ended. She packed all of her husband's belongings and gave them to Goodwill. She removed all the liquor from the house and destroyed every picture she could find of her husband. She was purging her life of the bad memories.

She even wanted to throw out the recliner her husband had spent so many nights in, drinking himself into a rage. But Dennis begged her not to do it. He needed to keep one last memory of his father.

A peaceful period emerged in the Collins household after Ron's death. No more yelling, no more drinking, no more beatings. Life became normal for the brothers. Dennis stopped wetting the bed. He stopped rocking back and forth to fall asleep, and stopped hiding under the covers. Normal conversations took place. Laughter returned. Whispering stopped, and normal voices were used. Memories of their father's beatings stopped appearing in their nightmares. Hope replaced fear. Laughter replaced crying. Things were good for a while. It would only last about a year.

Dennis didn't know it, but his mother was lonely. She

had been dependent on men her whole life, first her father, then her husband. She needed another man in her life. The problem was that she was a poor judge of character. Abusive men with drinking problems were like a magnet to Jane. She knew they were bad, knew they would hurt her. She just couldn't help it. They were the type of men she was attracted to.

At first, they were all kind to her. But eventually the abuse would start, verbal abuse at first, but always followed by physical abuse. Normally the real terror didn't begin until they moved into the house.

Jane was an attractive woman. She'd, married young and kept her youthful look into her early forties. Thick dark hair hung down to her shoulders and framed her face nicely. She had youthful, tanned skin with a face that was full of natural beauty. Jane was beautiful even without make-up, but with a little touch up she was stunning. Her body was not thin, but well-proportioned; Her eyes, perhaps her best quality, were deep blue and intoxicating. She attracted men like a picnic attracts flies.

The bars were her hunting ground. Jane wasn't much of a drinker, but she found the bar stool to be her quickest and most successful way to get male attention. She never had any trouble picking up a man. The problem was that she wasn't looking for just any man. With marriage on her mind, married men were of no interest to her. Young men weren't either. She was looking for older men, divorced men, men that had solid jobs — men that had money. Those men were difficult to find. Jane accepted a lot of free drinks, talked to a lot of men, and fought off a lot of advances, looking for the right man.

When she found one that met her needs, Jane moved quickly, like a spider that trapped men in her web. She fell in love fast and completely. Her passion escalated so quickly that she frightened many of the good men off — but never the bad men. Jane had some sort of perverted chemistry with bad men. Once they had a taste of her, they wouldn't leave. They could use and abuse her. She was powerless to stop them. They treated her like garbage, but she couldn't leave them.

Tom was the first man she brought home after her husband's death. Dennis and Kevin knew right away that he was a mirror image of their father. He drank until he could barely walk. The man was verbally abusive to Jane. He called her a whore and swore at her constantly. It didn't take long for Jane to realize he had lied about his job. Tom was unemployed, and had drank most of his savings.

When they first met, Tom told her that he was in sales, owned his own house, and made nearly a hundred thousand dollars per year. Jane thought he was well-heeled. But even after discovering the reality of Tom, she couldn't leave him. He was dependent on her money. She was dependent on his company. All Jane had known in life was abusive men. She knew no better.

Within a month of moving in, the verbal abuse turned violent. He began beating Jane. Dennis began hiding underneath the covers again. He rocked back and forth at night and wet the bed. The nightmares started all over again.

Kevin was the only strong one in the family. He wasn't afraid of Tom — he wasn't afraid of anything. He was disgusted with his mother's weakness, so much so that a hatred of her began to take hold inside him.

"She's a stupid, weak bitch," he told Dennis. "She deserves what she gets."

The brother was upset with Dennis's weakness too, but it was different. They were close. He felt sorry for his brother. Kevin didn't blame Dennis for his weakness. He didn't like it, but he understood it. His mother had made Dennis weak. She was to blame. It was Kevin's job to protect his brother. After all, no one else would.

As the beatings intensified and Dennis withdrew farther inside his shell, Kevin decided it was time to do something. Their mother's boyfriend had to go. One early morning after the violence stopped and everyone else was asleep, Kevin went into the garage, grabbed a container of anti-freeze, and brought it into the kitchen. Then he went to the liquor cabinet, picked out a half-empty bottle of Jim Beam, Tom's bourbon of choice, and brought it into the kitchen. He used a funnel to carefully pour a few ounces of anti-freeze into the bottle. He shook the bottle to mix the anti-freeze.

The coloring is off, he thought to himself.

He went to the pantry and got a bottle of brown food coloring, then put drops of it into the Jim Beam bottle and mixed it until the color was just right. He cleaned the funnel and put everything back.

Jane's boyfriend loved his Jim Beam. He loved it so much that he could tell that the taste was off just slightly from the partly empty bottle. The bourbon had a hint of sweetness to it. It left a slightly bitter after-taste in his mouth.

Maybe I left it open too long last night or didn't close the top tightly, he thought.

He thought about pouring it out and opening a fresh

bottle, but that would be a waste of good liquor. Besides, he wouldn't even notice the difference in taste after the second or third glass.

Tom liked his Jim Beam straight and on the rocks. He drank it cold, and usually finished the glass long before the ice melted.

"Fill up my glass, Jane, and put fresh ice in it," he yelled after downing the first glass.

Jane sat in the kitchen waiting to be summoned by him. She always waited there, at the breakfast table, sipping iced tea and reading her *People* magazine. She didn't dare walk away in case he needed her. If she needed to go to the bathroom or check on the boys, she would do it just after replenishing his drink. That bought her a few minutes until he would need something else.

She didn't dare venture out of hearing range. It might send him into a rage if she didn't respond quickly to one of his requests.

Midway through his fourth glass of Jim Beam, his chest began to pound. It got heavy. His breathing became labored. Intense pain shot from his chest down his left arm. He dropped his drink and slumped over in the chair.

Jane ran to his side, and yelled for Dennis to call 911. The ambulance arrived twenty minutes later. It was too late. Jane's boyfriend was dead.

After the ambulance left, Kevin emptied the remaining contents of the Jim Beam bottle in the sink, washed out the bottle, and threw it in the trash.

"What did you do, Kevin?" Dennis asked him.

"I did what you wanted me to do. I did what you

couldn't do yourself, what needed to be done."

Dennis knew exactly what Kevin had done. He suspected he had done it before, to their father. He wasn't upset with his brother. Instead, he was proud of him. Dennis wished he could be strong like Kevin. He wished he'd had the courage to take care of his mother's boyfriend. But that was never going to happen. Dennis was weak and could never hurt anyone.

"Now go in and comfort your mother, Dennis. She needs you now. Do what you do best, make her feel better."

Dennis's bond with his mother grew stronger after that night, while Kevin's relationship with her grew farther apart. While Dennis felt comfort in the time he spent with his mother, Kevin's despise for her weakness intensified. He couldn't stand to be around her. He spent most of his time away from home. When he did come home, he went into the basement, avoiding his mother as much as possible. One day, he moved his bed and all his belongings down to the basement.

"I'm sorry, bro," he told Dennis. "I love you, but I can't stand her. When she comes into the bedroom at night to give you a goodnight kiss, when she wakes you up in the morning, it makes my skin crawl. I can't stand seeing her anymore. I'm afraid I might do something terrible to her. I thinks it's best that I move to the basement. She won't go down there since Father fell down the stairs. I can avoid her as much as possible down there. Besides, she doesn't need me. She just needs you. You know she'd be happier if I left home and never came back. I can't do that now. I will someday soon, but for now, I'll stay in the basement. That's best for all of us."

Dennis tried to talk his brother out of it, but it was no use. When Kevin set his mind on doing something, no one was going to talk him out of it.

From that day on, Kevin rarely left the basement. He would come up and get food when his mother was asleep. He had all the basic necessities in that basement. Their father had installed a bathroom with a shower and sink. There was a bedroom in one corner, and there was even a small refrigerator and a television. Dennis went to the basement every day, sometimes for just a few minutes, other times for hours or until his mother needed him. His relationship with Kevin grew stronger. He could tell Kevin anything. He would listen and give advice. Dennis was as dependent on Kevin as he was on his mother.

As their mother's boyfriends came and went, Kevin was there for his brother. When one of their mother's boyfriends became violent, Dennis would find some excuse to get the boyfriend to go into the basement. Once downstairs, Kevin would convince him to go away. They always went away. Kevin was very convincing.

When each relationship ended, their mother would be sad. She would swear off men, and life in the Collins house would be good for a while. But Jane would eventually return to the bars and find another man. She couldn't help herself. Only age and fading looks slowed their mother's accumulation of men.

She married three more times after Ron's death. Each had some money. Each had even more life insurance. They all died, two from heart attacks, and one the result of a car accident. Jane was a very unlucky woman. But her ex-husbands' life insurance and savings all left Jane better off than she was coming into the marriage. Dennis comforted his mother during each grieving period. Kevin did not.

Kevin remained in the basement. Dennis would come down and spend time with him every day after school and whenever his mother didn't need him on weekends. He brought him food. They watched television together, played cards, and when Kevin took up a new hobby, Dennis helped him any way he could. Kevin's hobby was of no real interest to Dennis. He found it a little morbid, a little disturbing. But he was desperate to strengthen his relationship with his brother, so he pretended it was a hobby he was interested in too.

Taxidermy was not something Dennis was interested in. His father had taken it up as a hobby several years earlier, and had shown several of his finished projects to Dennis. They made him feel uneasy. He was surprised his brother found so much pleasure in displaying dead animals. But there were very few interests the two brothers shared, and Dennis was committed to put as much enthusiasm as possible into his brother's new hobby. He was desperate for Kevin's attention and approval.

Finding dead animals to use to develop his taxidermy skills proved to be more difficult than either boy thought.

"Birds must die all the time," Kevin told his brother. "But where do they go when they die? I never see them lying on the ground."

Most of the dead animals the boys spotted were roadkill, damaged too much to make them look alive again.

Finally, Kevin had an idea for getting fresh, dead animals and birds.

"I'll buy a high-powered BB gun and kill them myself," he said.

Every day for a couple of weeks, Dennis took a little bit of money from his mother's purse, not enough that she would miss it. When the boys had enough cash, they went to Walker's sporting goods store and bought a Crossman Air Pistol. Mr. Walker said it was the most powerful BB gun he had.

It took quite a bit of practice before Kevin killed his first prey, a small blue bird. With time, he became quite deadly with his pistol. When he got tired of birds, he moved to squirrels, then to ducks on the local pond. Eventually, he moved onto cats. They were extremely challenging for Kevin. They didn't die easily. Sometimes he would need to shoot them several times before they went down.

By the time the boys graduated from high school, the basement resembled a sort of menagerie of dead animals. Their mother had no idea of the boy's hobby. She never asked what they did in the basement, and she never went downstairs. She couldn't bear to go down there since her husband fell down the stairs.

The time came during the summer after high school graduation that Kevin would leave the house for good. He had planned to leave sooner but had stayed because of Dennis. He knew that Dennis needed him. He was a loner. All Dennis had in the world was his mother and brother. He had no friends. Kevin knew if he left, his mother would have complete influence over Dennis. Kevin couldn't allow that to happen. She was weak. She was needy. Dennis would never be strong enough to go out on his own as long as his mother had control of him.

So, when it was time for him to leave, Kevin sat down with his brother to talk about the future.

"Dennis, I've decided to go to mortuary school. I've got to do something with my life. I can't live in this house any longer. The local junior college has a two-year program. I can get an embalming license and go to work for a funeral home or crematory. It's kind of a natural transition for me from taxidermist to embalmer."

"When are you leaving, Kevin?"

"Tomorrow. Dennis, I want you to come with me. We can share a room. We can both learn a trade and get out of this house for good."

"I want to, Kevin. I really do. But I can't leave Mother. Her health is deteriorating. Her mind is starting to go, and I'm all she has. I just can't leave her."

Kevin was afraid that was what his brother would say. He had not been successful in pulling his brother away from their mother. He would never be successful. He realized that now.

The next morning before Dennis woke up, Kevin left the house for good. He knew Dennis would be upset. But he felt it was better to rip the Band-Aid off rather than let the pain of his leaving linger.

It would be weeks before he saw Dennis again. It was an accidental meeting. Dennis had come to the junior college. He was considering taking night classes, once or twice a week.

Mother would be fine without me for a couple of hours a week, he thought.

In the cafeteria that day, Dennis spotted his brother

sitting at a table by himself.

"Hello, Kevin. How are you doing?"

"Fine, bro, living the life, you know. What are you doing here, Dennis?"

"I thought I'd check out some evening classes, maybe one or two a week. Just enough to experience college life a little bit."

"Are you sure Mother will let you do that?"

"I don't plan on telling her, Kevin. I don't think she'll miss me for an hour or so in the evening. Besides, if I take an 8 p.m. class, she'll be asleep. She's going to bed around seven now. She's in poor health, Kevin. You should visit her."

"No fucking way, little bro. She's got you. That's all she needs. Hell, she probably doesn't even remember me, and I sure as hell am trying to forget her."

"Okay, Kevin. I understand. But there is no reason you and I shouldn't spend more time together. I miss you."

"Well, I tell you what, Dennis. I think that would be a good idea, and I think I know how we could do that and not take you away from Mother."

"How?"

"I need to make some money. Fact is, I'm broke. I've found a place that will take my animals on consignment — I took a few from the basement before I left. They've sold already. I've got more at the house. How about if I start coming over after Mother goes to bed? You can leave the back door unlocked. I can go into the basement and work on more projects to sell. I'll even cut you in for a portion of what I sell. You can come downstairs and visit me whenever you want. I'll leave the basement before Mother wakes up. She'll never know I'm down there."

"That sounds good to me, Kevin. When do you want to start coming over?"

"Tonight. All you need to do is unlock the back door once Mother has gone to sleep, and I'll slip in quietly and go down to the basement. Oh, and bro, I need a little cash to buy material to get started. How about if you lift a little money from Mother's purse, maybe a little bit at a time for a couple of weeks. That should give me enough seed money to get started."

"Okay, Kevin."

CHAPTER 5
THE BASEMENT

Dennis did whatever Kevin told him to do. He was willing to do whatever it took to rebuild his relationship with Kevin and still take care of his mother. Those nights in the basement were some of the best times in his life. Mother was asleep. They could talk, work, and make plans for the future. They stayed up until the wee hours of the morning, working on dead animals, giving them the appearance of life. Kevin became a skilled taxidermist. Dennis became his dependable assistant. Mother never knew what went on in the basement. She never asked, and Dennis never talked about it. Dennis never went down to the basement before his mother was asleep, and he was always upstairs before she woke up the next morning.

As his embalming training progressed, so did Kevin's interest in larger, more challenging animals to apply his taxidermy trade. At school, he had to follow the rules. His embalming was controlled. The school used unclaimed bodies from the city morgue to practice on. When Kevin became more skilled, he was able to assist embalmers at several of the local funeral homes. But still, there were limits to what he was able to do. He had to conform to what his instructor wanted.

Kevin had a talent that was not being realized. He was an artist with the dead. He knew he could give them more life than the embalming table would allow. Families wanted their loved ones to resemble what they remembered them looking like. They weren't interested in improvement. They weren't interested in making their loved one more attractive in death than they were in life. Kevin's talents were being wasted as an embalmer.

But no one was telling him what to do in the basement. He was free to use all his creativity. He was free to be an artist.

When he graduated from mortuary school, Kevin went to work for a local funeral home, Light Family Funeral Home. Daniel Light, the owner, started him out as a funeral director. He worked visitations in the evening and helped with funerals. But Kevin was not a social person. He was uncomfortable around people, and families were uncomfortable around him. After a short period, Kevin moved down to the embalming room. He made body pick-ups and worked the graveyard shift embalming bodies. Most of the time he was alone. That suited him fine.

On his off-nights, Kevin went to the basement. His brother would be waiting for him. Dennis would scavenge for unique, larger specimens for Kevin to apply his skills. Each week he would have a different project waiting for Kevin. Some, when finished, were given to the consignment store and sold. Others, Kevin's best and most challenging work, was never sold. Those creations remained in the basement for he and Dennis to treasure.

The basement, in time, became a menagerie of Kevin's work. Dead animals and creatures of all sizes found their final resting place in that basement. No one came into that basement except Kevin and Dennis. No one would understand what was down there.

One morning after Dennis had finished breakfast, the doorbell rang. A policeman was standing there.

"Hello, Officer," Dennis said. "What can I do for you?"

"We're investigating the disappearance of a woman and several pets. I am talking to everyone in the neighborhood. Have you seen this woman?" the officer asked, holding out a picture of a slender, silver-haired woman who looked to be in her eighties.

"No, I don't believe so, Officer? Who is she?"

"Her name is Mary Brown. She lives about a mile down the road. She disappeared two nights ago along with her dog, a yellow lab named Henry. Are you certain you haven't seen them?"

"No, I haven't seen them."

"Have you seen anything unusual in the area? Pets that look like they were taken against their will, someone prowling through the area, anything suspicious?"

"No, Officer, I haven't."

The officer took out a notepad and a pen and began to scribble notes. "What is your name, young man?"

"Dennis Collins, sir."

"Does anyone else live here, Mr. Collins?"

"Yes, my mother."

"I'd like to speak to her. Is she home?"

"Yes, Officer, but I'm afraid she is not feeling well. She's in bed, sleeping now."

"Okay, Dennis. But could you please give her my card and ask her to call me as soon as she can?"

"Yes, I'll do that."

Once he left, Dennis went to his mother's room and quietly opened the door. "Are you awake, Mother?"

"Yes dear. Who was at the door?"

"No one really, Mother. It was just a salesman. I'm sorry he rang the doorbell. I'll put a note on the door so if anyone else comes, they won't disturb you."

Dennis put a note on the door asking not to be disturbed. Then he locked and deadbolted the front door and did the same to the rear door. He pulled all the curtains and turned out the lights. Then he went down to the basement.

I will need to talk to Kevin tonight, he thought. *We need to be more careful. We can't have the police coming around.*

Dennis was always the more careful brother. Yet, this time, it was he that made the mistake.

Kevin will not be happy with me, Dennis thought.

The basement was dark, cold, and damp. There were puddles in several areas of the floor along the concrete wall, where the heavy rain from the night before had fallen through the cracks and puddled in the low-lying areas of the basement floor. The basement was old. The concrete used to pour the floor had buckled and settled, causing uneven patches.

When he was young and wanted to hide from his father, he would go down to the basement. After heavy rains, there would always be puddles. He would take his plastic ships and his plastic army men, float the ships in the puddle, and pretend the army was invading the dry land surrounding the puddle. He had watched invasions of soldiers from oceans many times on television.

His father had served in the marines many years earlier. He enjoyed war movies, and when his father was reasonably sober and in a good mood, Dennis would sit next to him and watch the movies too. Those were some of the few good memories he had of his father.

At the bottom of the basement stairs, Dennis pulled the chain dangling below a single eighty-watt light bulb. The light illuminated only a small portion of the basement. Kevin didn't like a lot of light. He preferred working amongst the shadows of his creatures.

"Besides, the darkness makes it difficult for the curious to look into the basement from the windows leading outside," Kevin would say.

The problem is that even with little light, someone could spy on the basement through those windows, Dennis thought.

Dennis couldn't take that chance now that the police were snooping around. He took old blankets from a storage container and hung them over the three basement windows.

"That should do the trick," he said to himself.

With the windows covered, the only light in the basement came from that one eighty-watt light bulb. Day looked like night.

Dennis had grown accustomed to working at night, with little light. He felt comfortable in the quiet darkness of that basement.

In one corner was a bedroom. It had a small cot to lay

on, a refrigerator, and a bathroom. On a nightstand next to the cot was a small lamp. Dennis flipped on the light and closed the bedroom door. This had been Kevin's room during the years he lived in the basement. It was simple and plain, but it served a purpose. In the corner of the room was a space heater. Dennis had taken it from his mother's room years earlier. She had several, and he figured she would never miss it. He was right, too. She never asked about it.

The room was cold. The space heater helped at night. At least, that's what Kevin said. Dennis had never slept in that room.

The nights that Kevin came home to work in the basement, he would often sleep in that room after he finished with one of his projects. He rarely slept more than two or three hours at a time, just long enough to get a little rest. He was always gone by the time the sun came up.

Dennis stocked the refrigerator with food and drinks for his brother. He was always hungry after he finished with one of his projects.

The bathroom in the basement was rarely used. The toilet was not flushed, and the sink water was not turned on during the nights Kevin was home. The pipes leading from the sink, toilet, and bathtub were old and made a loud racket when water ran through them. Neither Dennis nor Kevin wanted to chance waking their mother, so the toilet was not flushed, and the sink water was not turned on during the night. On the rare occasions that Kevin needed to use the toilet, the contents would stay in the bowl until the next day, when Mother was awake.

Against one basement wall was a wood shelf spanning

the length of the wall, three shelves high to within a couple of feet of the basement ceiling. Ron Collins had used the shelves for storage, paint cans, old books, old memories, and seasonal items such as Christmas decorations.

Kevin and Dennis moved everything off the shelves onto a corner of the basement floor. The shelves now housed the smaller projects of Kevin's taxidermy skills. Birds of all types occupied one area. Squirrels and raccoons in another. Ducks and geese were in a separate area. Cats and small dogs were segregated in different areas on the shelves.

Kevin believed in an afterlife. He believed that some of his creations would come back to life.

"Not the same life we share," he would tell Dennis. "There is an alternate universe where the souls of some of God's creatures live on, even after death."

Kevin believed the skills he used as a taxidermist would preserve the bodies so they would appear, in the afterlife, as good as or better than they looked during their life on earth. Kevin also believed that not all God's creatures were destined for the afterlife. Only the ones that had lived a pure life would be permitted to live on.

Kevin had the skills and ability to identify those that were destined for a second life. Those creatures were the ones that occupied space in the basement. The ones that were not worthy were taken to the consignment shop or destroyed.

In a way, the basement was a sort of purgatory between death on earth and the afterlife. The creatures waited patiently and quietly for their spirits to be lifted and their souls to begin a new life. Kevin was the artist. Dennis was the caretaker.

Kevin instructed Dennis to segregate the creatures

into their own separate areas in the basement. He referred to those areas as communities. He believed that by keeping like creatures together in death, they would also be together in the afterlife. So, each species shared their own small community within the sanctuary of the basement shelves.

The larger of God's creatures were treated the same way. Each species occupied a different section of the basement floor. Dennis was instructed by his brother not to put creatures that fought in life close to each other.

"Those creatures need to occupy communities within a safe distance of each other so as not to be grouped together in the afterlife," Kevin said.

Communities of large dogs occupied one section of the basement floor far away from the cats' community. Likewise, birds were kept far apart from both the cat and dog communities.

The basement was a sanctuary for all God's creatures that Kevin deemed worthy of his skills. As such, they were treated with respect and care. Dennis spent hours every day talking to them, listening to them, caring for them. Those creatures became his friends. He loved them like he loved his mother and brother. They came alive when he was in the basement.

But not all the creatures in the basement enjoyed the company of Dennis. The fresh ones, the ones that were still alive, were frightened of him. They did not welcome death. They struggled to stay alive. They resisted Dennis.

"You don't understand," Dennis would tell them. "My brother is an artist. He will make you even more beautiful than you are now."

Dennis didn't want the living creatures in the basement to fear him. He tried to understand them. They had known nothing but this world, and had all suffered to some degree. Life had been hard for them. Death was not to be feared, it was to be cherished. It was no more than a bus stop on the road to a better world. Soon they would realize that. But for now, they feared what they didn't know.

Still, he cared for them just like he cared for the dead creatures in the basement. He gave them water and fed them. Dennis told them they had nothing to be afraid of. None believed him. Some made noise. He couldn't allow that. Mother was sleeping. Those creatures were given an injection to calm them, to help them sleep, to silence their voices.

At 11:30 a.m., every day, Dennis went upstairs into the kitchen. He would make lunch for his mother, himself, and the living guests down in the basement. It was always a simple lunch—a sandwich, a piece of fruit, and a drink, usually iced tea. Mother liked iced tea. It was her drink of choice ever since Dennis could remember. Mother didn't eat much, and neither did Dennis. The simple lunch suited them well.

As for the living creatures in the basement, they never seemed to have much of an appetite.

When the sandwiches were made, Dennis put his mother's meal on a tray and walked it into her room. She was usually asleep. He set her meal on the nightstand next to her and changed the television channel to *Matlock*. That was one of her favorite shows. It came on every day at noon, and was followed by *Murder She Wrote* and *Perry Mason*. Mother loved old dramas and mysteries.

After leaving her tray, Dennis took food down to the

basement. He opened up the cages where the living creatures stayed and placed the food trays next to them. Then, he walked back upstairs to eat his lunch. Dennis always ate his meals at the breakfast table. It was more a matter of habit than preference. He had been eating every meal his entire life at that breakfast table. Father insisted on it when he was alive. He would never permit food to be taken out of the kitchen. After his death, Mother held on to the same rule.

Partway through lunch, the phone rang.

"Dennis Collins?"

"Yes."

"Mr. Collins, this is Detective Baczenas with the Kansas City Police Department. I'm following up on a conversation you had with one of our officers a few days ago.

"Yes, Detective. What can I do for you?"

"Mr. Collins, I need to speak to your mother. Is she available to talk? It's very important that I speak to her."

"She's not feeling good today, Detective. I believe she is asleep."

"Please, Mr. Collins, can you check to see if she can come to the phone?"

"Yes, I'll check."

Dennis put the phone down and walked into his mother's bedroom. She was still asleep. The lunch tray was on her nightstand, untouched.

"Mother, wake up," he said, shaking her gently.

"What is it, Dennis?"

"Detective Baczenas is on the phone. He insists that he needs to speak with you right away."

"Okay," she said, reaching for the phone on the

nightstand. "What can I do for you, Detective?" she asked.

"Mrs. Collins?"

"Yes, what do you need, Detective?"

"I am investigating the disappearance of Mary Lou Brown. She's a neighbor of yours, in her eighties, with short silver hair and glasses. Do you know her?"

"No, I'm afraid not. Because of my health, I rarely leave the house."

"Well, Mrs. Collins, she disappeared from her house on Maple Street two nights ago. She lives about six blocks from you. I was wondering if you heard anything unusual that night, say between one and three?"

"No, I'm afraid I was sound asleep at that hour, and I'm a very sound sleeper."

"Well, thanks, Mrs. Collins? May I ask one other question, please?"

"Yes, Detective. What is it?"

"Do you know if your son was home that night?"

"What kind of question is that? Of course he was home. Dennis goes to sleep right after I do, and he never leaves me alone at night."

"Well, is it possible he slipped out of the house after you were asleep, Mrs. Collins?"

"Absolutely not, Detective. Ever since my health started to deteriorate, Dennis never leaves the house at night. Why would you think such a thing?"

"A neighbor of Mrs. Brown's saw a man about your son's age and build leaving the back yard of Mrs. Brown's house about the time she disappeared."

"Well, I can assure you, that person wasn't my son."

"Thanks, Mrs. Collins."

After she hung up the phone, his mother turned to Dennis. "You didn't leave the house the other night, did you?"

"No, Mother. I didn't."

"You're a good boy, Dennis."

"Thanks, Mother. I wish you would eat some of your food. You haven't eaten anything in a few days. I'm worried about you."

"Don't worry, Dennis. I'm fine, just tired—always tired. Leave the sandwich. I'll try to eat some in a little bit."

"Okay, Mother. Do you need anything else?"

"No, Dennis. I'm fine. Just turn out the light and hand me the channel changer before you go."

"Okay, Mother. If you need anything just ring the bell."

There was a bell on the nightstand that Dennis had placed there months earlier in case his mother needed him. The entire time it had been there, she never rang it. Dennis knew she wouldn't unless it was an emergency. That was good. He wasn't sure he would hear it in the basement anyway.

After leaving the bedroom, Dennis cleaned his dish and then went down to the basement again. He walked to the farthest corner of the basement, took a key out of his pocket, and unlocked a door to a small storage room. It was completely dark inside. Dennis pulled out a flashlight from his other pocket and turned it on. Inside were four large, wire dog cages, each covered with a blanket. He pulled the blanket off one at a time to examine his live specimens. Three were asleep. None had eaten their food. He left the food trays and went to the fourth cage.

That specimen was waking up. The drugs were

beginning to wear off.

"You should eat something," Dennis said. "I made you a sandwich."

The woman, groggy from the drugs, struggled to focus her eyes on the person that was talking.

"Where am I?" she said.

"You're in a safe place," Dennis said.

"Where is my dog?" she asked.

"He is safe too. He's taking a nap now."

"Please, I want to go home."

"You will," Dennis said. "Hopefully tonight."

"What do you want with me?"

"We want to help you."

"Then let me go," the old woman said.

"We will. But it's not your time yet. Please eat something. The sandwich is good. It's ham and cheese on wheat bread — Mother's favorite. Please eat. I'm going to need to give you something to help you sleep. It will take a few minutes to work. That should give you enough time to finish your sandwich."

"I'm not hungry. Please let me go. I won't tell anyone. I promise."

Dennis moved to a table sitting next to the cage and lifted a plastic juice bottle. He reached into his pocket and pulled out a plastic bag containing a white powder. He poured some of the contents into the plastic bottle and shook it. Then he handed it to the woman.

"No, I'm not thirsty," she said.

"Drink it, or I'll need to force you to," he said.

She took two small sips and handed the bottle back.

"I'm afraid you are going to need to drink more than that," he said, handing the bottle back to her.

She drank until Dennis motioned for her to stop.

"Good. Now eat that sandwich before you take another nap."

CHAPTER 6
KEVIN AND MARY

Kevin was angry that night when Dennis told him about Detective Baczenas.

"Dammit, Dennis. You've got to be more careful. We can't have the police suspicious of us. From now on, get our projects from the other side of town. Look around the railroad tracks and the homeless shelters. And make damn sure you aren't seen."

"But I'll need to use Mother's car to get to those areas."

"So what? She doesn't drive anymore."

"She won't like me taking her car."

"Make her one of your special drinks, Dennis. She'll sleep through the night and won't know a thing."

"But those areas are dangerous. I don't think I can do that."

"Geez, Dennis. You're nothing but a little wimp. Tell you what, give me the keys and I'll do it."

After that night, Kevin got his own specimens.

They took safeguards in the basement, too. The door leading to the basement was locked at all times. Blackout curtains were put on the basement windows. The door leading to the room with the cages was re-enforced and new, stronger locks were added. A new room was added with a secret door and locks. That room was used for the large specimens, after Kevin was finished with them. In that room, the dead waited for their trip to the afterlife. That room was for Kevin's greatest artistic work, the projects the outside world would not understand. On the off chance that someone was to come into the basement, that was a room they didn't want anyone to see.

Detective Baczenas' investigation of the disappearance of Mary Lou Brown stalled. Leads dried up, and eventually the case was put in the cold case files.

Dennis and Kevin were intertwined because of their hobby in the basement. That was the one part of both their lives that bonded them to each other.

But outside of the basement, they drifted further apart. Both wanted different things in life. Dennis was content taking care of his mother, living in the house where he grew up, sleeping in the same bedroom he had since he was a child. He didn't need more out of life. The outside world was not something he was interested in. He disliked people—in fact, he was uncomfortable around them. Life in that house was predictable, comfortable. Life outside the house was not. The times he left the house were few — to get groceries or medicine or some sort of incidental item that mother requested.

Kevin was the stronger of the two. He wasn't afraid of people—he despised most of them, but he wasn't afraid of them. He was confident around others. Kevin yearned for a wife and family. He wanted some sort of normality in his life. He was twenty-four when he dated for the first time, having met the woman in Kelly's bar. She was older than him by ten-years, having been married three times already with two children, both teenage girls. Marsha Thompson was experienced. She was a regular customer in the bar. Most men that frequented Kelly's knew her — many had slept with her. She was still married to her third husband at the time Kevin first dated her. He was not aware that she was married. She didn't wear a wedding band. It was more difficult to pick up men with a wedding band on her finger.

She spent her evenings in the bar when her husband, a long-haul truck driver, was out of town. Lately, he had been out of town a lot.

Kevin sat at a table in a dark corner of Kelly's. He liked to be left alone with a bottle of Old Crow and a cold draft every thirty minutes or so. Marsha had caught his eye on many occasions. She was loud, outgoing, and dressed like a hooker. He had wanted her for a long time, but had never acted on his urges. By the time he had enough liquid courage, she had already selected a man for the night's entertainment.

But this night was different. Perhaps she'd already had each of the men in the bar that night. Or perhaps she noticed Kevin looking at her from the other side of the room. Whatever the reason was, that night she walked over to his table and sat down. They talked, laughed, danced, and drank. The more they drank, the more they were attracted to each other. She wanted him to feel a little less lonely. He wanted her because she was a fantasy he had never realized. They left the bar at closing time. She took his hand and led him to a vacant piece of ground, hidden behind the dumpsters at the side of the bar. On that dirty, gravel piece of ground, she gave herself to him.

Marsha was the first woman that had shown any interest in Kevin. He couldn't get enough of her. She tried to push him away, had countless affairs with other men. She did what she wanted and took whoever she wanted. He sat quietly in that bar, night after night, waiting for her. If the selection of men was slim or not up to her standards, she would take Kevin to the parking lot or woods behind the bar, or inside her car. He was her choice when there was nothing better.

One night, her husband came home unexpectedly and came to Kelly's looking for his wife. She was on the dance floor with a young man. Mary liked younger men. She was rubbing up against him during a slow dance and they were kissing—long, slow, passionate kisses. Kevin watched from his table as her husband hurried onto the dance floor. With one punch, he laid the young man out on the dance floor. Max Thompson was a large man, tall, heavy set and muscular. He was angrier than Mary had ever seen him. He grabbed Mary's arm and pulled her off the dance floor, then dragged her out into the parking lot. He tried to pull her into his pick-up truck. She resisted. He began to hit her. With each blow, she resisted more. She tried to fight back but he was much stronger than her. Three more punches and she fell to the ground. She was in too much pain to resist anymore. Her husband bent over to pick her up from the ground just as the tire iron clobbered him over the back of his head. The first whack only angered him more. The second whack dazed him. The third whack knocked him out.

Kevin helped Mary off the ground and to her car. "Was that your husband?" he asked.

"Yes."

"I don't think you should go home, Mary."

"I've got to. I have two daughters there. I can't leave them alone with him."

"Don't worry. I'll have a talk with your husband. I don't think he'll bother you again."

Max Thompson didn't bother his wife or children again. His pick-up truck went over the edge of a large hill overlooking Lake Covington. It tumbled a hundred feet down the hill into the lake. His body was found in the cab of his pick-up truck the next day. His blood-alcohol level was three times the legal limit. His death was ruled an accident.

Three months later Marsha and Kevin were married. The life insurance on her late husband was substantial, enough to buy the couple a comfortable, two story home.

Marsha was never a faithful wife, and she never would be. But she needed a man, a husband, someone that made her feel safe. Someone to keep her company during her lonely nights. Kevin provided her with that.

For months after their wedding, Kevin lived a normal life. He worked and came home to his family. His drinking slowed and he tried to be a good husband and father. During that time, Kevin stayed away from his brother and the basement. Marsha changed too, for a while. Down deep, she wanted a normal life. She wanted to be loved by one man. She wanted to be a good wife and mother. Or maybe both of them just thought that was what they wanted.

Neither was capable of destroying their demons. They could only bury them for a short time. Marsha was the first to allow her dark side to return.

She told Kevin she needed a break from the kids — she needed a girl's night out to spend the evening with her girlfriends. Kevin didn't know it then, but Marsha had no girlfriends. His wife had no interest in befriending other women. They were competition. Marsha didn't want the attention she would get to be shared with others. In the back of his mind, Kevin knew what his wife had planned that evening by the way she was dressed — halter-top, no bra, and mini-skirt, with one-inch high-heels. She was going hunting along the barstools of Kelly's Tavern. Still, Kevin wanted to trust her. He wanted to believe her night out would be innocent.

Kevin sat in his recliner, watched football, and drank beer. The girls were in their rooms, like they always were.

Marsha's daughters are impossible to figure out, he thought.

They rarely said anything to him. Sometimes they would go days without even talking to him. If they needed something, they asked their mom. It was as if he didn't exist at all.

Maybe it's because they're teenagers, he thought. *But more than likely it's because they haven't had a stable father figure in their lives before.*

After four beers, Kevin opened up a new bottle of Old Crow. The beer gave him a buzz. The whiskey would deliver him to his happy place. But that night, it only made him more suspicious of his wife's intentions. The more he drank, the angrier he got. He never got to a happy place that night.

When Marsha arrived home, it was a few minutes past

4 a.m. She reeked of booze. Her lipstick and make-up were smeared.

Kevin began screaming at her. "You whore. You've been with some other guy, haven't you?" he said, slurring his words and trying to get up from his chair.

"So what?" she said. "You're in no shape to take care of me. Sometimes I need a real man, not a fucking wimp like you."

Kevin raised his hand. He wanted to hit her, but he was too drunk. He took one step toward her and fell on the floor.

"You're too fucking drunk to even slap me. I don't know why I married you. You're pathetic," she said, laughing at him.

That was the beginning of the end of civility in their marriage. The love was gone after that night. Maybe it was never there to begin with. They would grow to hate each other. But for some reason that defied logic, they stayed together. Perhaps it was because neither wanted to be alone. Or perhaps it was because angry sex got both of them excited. They would scream at each other. They would hit each other. They were physically violent toward each other. Both came close to killing the other. But when the abuse ended, they shared rough, angry sex. They hated each other, but they were addicted to each other.

After that first brutal fight, Kevin's drinking increased. He drank each night until he could barely stand. Then, the violence began. He was becoming his father. But Marsha was nothing like his mother. She was every bit as violent as he was, their fights often resulting in the police being called.

Kevin left the house for weeks at a time. During those periods, he stayed in the basement of his mother's house. Dennis was glad to see his brother again, even though this version of Kevin was more angry and violent than ever before. The projects in the basement resumed. But the specimens Kevin brought into the business changed. They were all young, attractive women. They dressed provocatively. They wore heavy make-up. They had long, dark hair. They all resembled Kevin's wife in some fashion.

He found them on streets and in bars in different parts of the city. None lived close by—he wasn't going to make that mistake again. Kevin hunted for his specimens at night, after work. When he chose one, he used chloroform to subdue them, put them in the trunk of his car, and drove to his mother's house. Dennis unlocked the back door every night after Mother went to sleep, in anticipation that his brother would come home.

Belinda was his first specimen after he returned to the basement. She was a prostitute, walking the two blocks between an X-rated movie theatre and a strip-joint at nearly 4 a.m. She was near the end of her shift, and hadn't had a customer for nearly an hour. But Johnny, her boyfriend and pimp, insisted she work until an hour before the sun came up. Kevin had spotted her before—he had watched her for several nights. She wasn't the only streetwalker that worked that area. But she stayed on the streets later than the others. He knew when her potential clients went home. He knew when Johnny would come to pick her up. He knew when no one would be around.

Tonight was the night. He had already decided that. He

sat parked a block away in a dark parking lot. Kevin scanned the area for witnesses. He didn't see anyone. So, he started the engine, turned on his lights, and drove slowly up the block until he spotted Belinda walking. He pulled up next to her. She turned and smiled at him.

"Do you want a date, hun?" she asked.

"Maybe. How much?" he asked.

She walked over to the car. "Are you a cop?" she asked.

"No, are you?" Kevin asked.

She smiled, and pulled down her top just far enough to expose her breasts.

"No, hun. I'm not. Thirty for a blow. Sixty for half and half, and a hundred for around the world."

"Thirty is all I can afford," he said.

"Too bad. I could really rock your world tonight, hun."

Kevin unlocked the door and she got in. He scanned the area one more time for any witnesses.

"What's the matter, hun? There's no need to be nervous. I won't bite — unless you want me to, that is."

"Where should we go?" Kevin asked.

"First, give me the thirty."

He reached in his wallet and pulled out a twenty and a ten.

"Go two blocks down and turn right. There's a quiet street there."

He went where she told him and parked the car.

She reached over to unzip his pants. "Wow. You are excited to see me, aren't you, hun?" She began to stroke him with her right hand while she licked the tip of his dick, soft gentle licks. "Now, don't come in my mouth, hun. You didn't pay for that. When you get ready to shoot, tell me and I'll massage you until you come."

It took only a few seconds for Kevin to reach full erection. His rod began throbbing. Belinda could feel the passion rising. She took all his rod into her mouth, with long quick movements of her lips. Kevin began to shake with excitement.

"I'm coming," he hollered.

Belinda took his meat deep into her mouth one last time and then pulled her lips back to his tip, waiting for his juices to surge. When she felt them coming, she pulled her mouth away and massaged his rod with both hands, squeezing the juices onto the seat of the car. She was still squeezing when the cloth soaked in chloroform was forced into her face. She struggled to remove his hand, but it was no use. Thirty seconds later she had passed out.

Kevin lifted her from the car seat and placed her in the trunk. He drove to his mother's house, watching the rearview mirror all the way to make sure he wasn't followed.

When he got to the house, he scanned the area for anyone that might be watching. When he saw no one, he popped the trunk and lifted his specimen. Kevin carried her to the back of the house. The rear door was unlocked. He opened it, then carried her inside and down to the basement.

Dennis was waiting downstairs. "Hey, bro, what did you bring us tonight?"

"Her name is Belinda. Take good care of her until I'm ready. She's special. I want her to stay fresh. Feed her, give her plenty of water, and let her rest. I've got special plans for her."

Dennis was the caregiver. Kevin was the artist. Dennis kept the future projects alive and reasonably healthy until his artist brother was ready to apply his craft.

Belinda was the only occupant in the cages in the special room in the corner of the basement. There would be others later, but not while Belinda was there. She bore a remarkable likeness to Marsha, right down to the slutty clothes she wore. Every night, Kevin brought a change of clothes into the basement. Each outfit was from Marsha's closet, the trashiest, sexiest, sluttiest outfits Kevin could find. Each one had been worn by his wife when they had made love at one time or another. Each one had been worn by his wife when she went trolling for other men. Kevin had both a love and hate relationship with each of the outfits he brought into the basement for Belinda to wear. Each outfit got him excited, but each outfit reminded him of how his wife used them to lure her new lovers.

Dennis prepared Belinda every evening for Kevin's arrival. He bathed her, he applied her make-up, he dressed her in the clothes Kevin had brought the night before. All the preparation was done while Belinda was numbed by sleeping pills.

"She'll be much more cooperative that way," Kevin told his brother.

Medication was last given to Belinda around five. By the time Kevin arrived, the medication was beginning to wear off. That's what Kevin wanted. He wanted her awake, wanted her to see him. Kevin wanted to see the fear in her eyes. He wanted to hear her voice begging him to let her go, begging him not to hurt her. Kevin and Dennis even added extra insulation and sound-proofing material to the walls and ceiling of the special room so Mother wouldn't hear the screaming.

Kevin liked to inflict pain on Belinda. With her, he was able to do what he couldn't do to his wife. He was free to use any creative means he desired to get the gratification he could no longer get from Marsha.

Belinda suffered, but none of her wounds were visible. Kevin made sure of that. She was too perfect of a specimen to damage.

When he was done with her for the evening, Dennis provided her medication to sleep. He bandaged her, if needed, cleaned her up, brought her a late-night snack before the medication took hold, and changed the sheets and covers in her cage. Dennis was the caregiver.

Dennis was not like Kevin. He got no enjoyment from hurting people. But he understood his brother. He understood his needs and understood his sickness. He helped his brother because he loved him, because the basement was the only thing they had in common anymore.

Belinda remained a prisoner in the basement for nearly three months. Finally, one night, Kevin's creative juices returned. He was ready to prepare Belinda for her afterlife. He instructed Dennis to prepare a table in the room in the basement near the cages. She was drowsy but awake when Kevin pulled her out of the cage and strapped her down to the table, kicking and screaming when he inserted the device in her veins. Her eyes began to bulge as the machine sucked blood from her body. Kevin had used the machine many times in the embalming process, but that was different. Those were corpses — they couldn't feel any pain. They couldn't show any fear. This time, his subject was alive. This time, he could see the pain in her face. This time he could listen to her screams.

A rush of excitement, greater than anything he had ever experienced, ran through his body. He wanted it to last as long as possible. But that turned out not to be long at all. Belinda passed out within five minutes, and was dead in ten. The rapid removal of blood had sent her into shock, then shortly after, taken her life.

She would be his finest work. In death, she would look exactly like Marsha. In death, she would be a permanent resident of the basement. She would reside in a special place in the basement, a shrine to Kevin's creative genius.

CHAPTER 7
DARK MINDS

Belinda's screams during the last minutes of her life were deafening, but Mother didn't hear a word. She slept through the noises that came from the basement. The extra insulation and sound proofing material Dennis and Kevin had added to the basement walls and ceiling helped. The large dose of sleeping pills Dennis put in his mother's nighttime tea worked even better.

Mother always had a steaming cup of Earl Grey tea, with a slice of lemon and a teaspoon of honey, just before she went to sleep. Dennis brought it to her every night at precisely eight-thirty. A half hour later she was sound asleep.

There were things that went on in that house late at night that Mother wouldn't approve of. She was such a prim and proper lady, naïve to the dark side that resided in the people she loved. Dennis was her protector. He was her caregiver. He never allowed her to see the dark side of his brother. For all she knew, Kevin had disappeared long ago.

She never heard him enter the house, and she never saw him. The drugs mixed inside her night time tea assured that.

Even during the years after her husband died, when she had lovers that resided in the house, she was not aware of the evil that took place late at night. Her night time tea protected her innocence. She was beautiful back then, and had no trouble attracting men. The problem was that she always attracted the wrong men. Her body was a magnet for damaged, hateful, violent men that used and abused women for their own sick pleasure. She attracted men similar to Ron Collins. They were mean drunks. They had no respect for women. Most were unemployed or worked only occasionally. None made a decent living. All lived off Jane's generosity and Ron Collins's life insurance proceeds. None would be missed when they disappeared.

Earl Chase watched as Jane walked into Kelly's tavern one cold, wintery night. The snow had been falling all evening, the temperature outside nearly zero. It was a nasty night to be outside, but a good night to be in Kelly's. The beer was cold, the music was loud, and the women were plentiful. Problem was that Earl had a bit of a nasty reputation with many of the regular women customers. Most avoided him, the attractive ones anyway. They saw him for what he was—a drunk with a bad attitude and no future.

Jane took a seat at the bar. She had not been in Kelly's for nearly a year, since her last relationship ended. None of the customers in Kelly's that night recognized her. She'd had success sitting at that bar before. It was, as one of the male customers had told her, "the area where women that wanted to be picked up sat."

Jane wanted to be picked up. She was lonely. It had been a long time since she had a man in her bed. She had sworn off them after her last abusive relationship.

"I'm done with men. All that is important in this world is us. I don't need anyone else," she told Dennis a year earlier when her last abusive boyfriend disappeared.

Dennis knew she didn't mean it—she never did. He understood his mother better than she understood herself. She needed a man in her life. She could go awhile without one, but eventually she would return to Kelly's.

Earl watched her as she took off her coat and set it on the bar stool next to her. Her legs were long, thin, and sexy. Her dress was red, short, and fit tightly against her perfect body. Two thin straps connected the front of the dress to the rear, showing perfectly tanned skin from her neck to her breasts. Earl knew the second she walked in the bar that he had to have her.

"Bartender, give me another, and give the lady in red a glass of champagne on me."

As the bartender poured the champagne, Earl made his move. He slid onto the bar stool next to Jane, removing her coat from the seat and setting it on the stool next to him.

"Do you mind if I sit here?" he asked.

"No, it's fine," she said, giving him a quick glance and a brief smile.

The bartender set a frosty mug of draft beer in front of Earl, and a glass of champagne in front of Jane.

"The champagne is compliments of the gentleman next to you," the bartender said.

"Well, thank you, sir," she said to Earl with a smile on

her face.

"A beautiful drink for a beautiful lady." He winked. "My name is Earl," he said, holding out his hand.

"Nice to meet you, Earl. I'm Jane," she said, shaking his hand.

Earl was not the type of man she would normally be interested in. He was older, in his fifties. He had balding hair, brown with gray scattered throughout. He was heavy-set with a large beer-belly, the result of too much beer and too little exercise. Jane was not physically attracted to him. But loneliness and several more glasses of champagne would change that.

They kissed on the dance floor an hour later. They had sex in the cab of his pick-up truck thirty minutes after that. Jane was the most beautiful, sexy woman Earl had ever been with. She was classy and educated, not like the trailer park trash he normally picked up. Jane was way out of his league and he knew it. He took her quickly on the cold, cloth bench seat of his cab. She barely had time to remove her coat and pantyhose before he pushed inside her. Three quick thrusts and it was over. Jane didn't even have time to warm up.

Sex wasn't a priority for Jane—she didn't enjoy it. It was a means to an end for her. Men wanted sex. She gave it to them to keep them. In all her years, she had never made love, and she never had love made to her. The type of men she attracted weren't interested in taking the time to please a woman. They were only interested in immediate gratification. She gave that to them.

Jane often fantasized about having a man that completely satisfied her; a man that kissed her tenderly with soft, warm, sober lips. A man that touched her gently in all the right places; a man that took his time to make love, making sure she was completely satisfied before taking care of himself. She had seen it on television and in movie theatres. She had read about it in love novels. But she had never experienced it. Jane had never had an orgasm that she didn't initiate herself.

Jane had no reason to like men. They had only hurt her. "Slam, bam, thank you ma'am," was the story of her love life. That wasn't likely to change based on the type of men she attracted in Kelly's tavern.

Earl seemed different from the others. He was caring, he listened to Jane, and took her to restaurants, not just to bed. Earl had a job—not much of one, but he had one—and as a result he had some money to spend on her. Drinking was not a priority in his life. He liked drinking, but he didn't need it.

She was not physically attracted to him. When they had sex, she closed her eyes and fantasized about other men. But after the first night in the cab of his truck, he made an effort. He showed that he cared and showed that he wanted more than just sex. Earl was persistent, and he made her feel she was special. For those reasons, the relationship lasted.

Two months after they first met, he proposed to her. Two days later, he moved into the house.

Jane's relationship with Earl was different from any other she'd had. He helped around the house, cooked dinner, and washed dishes. And he was kind to Dennis.

He probably would treat Kevin with kindness too if he ever came out of the basement, Dennis thought.

Jane never talked about Kevin. It was as if he never existed. Dennis was the one that told Earl his brother lived in the basement. When Earl tried to talk to Jane about her other son, she got angry and refused to talk about him.

"He died years ago," she said. "And I don't want to talk about him."

But as Earl's relationship with Dennis warmed up, he confided more about his brother to him.

"Mother doesn't love him anymore. She doesn't want him in the house. You mustn't talk about him to her, and you must swear you'll never tell her that her son is living in the basement. Mother would be angry."

Earl's curiosity about Kevin grew. The times he was alone with Dennis, he would ask about his brother. Most of the time, Dennis was guarded and refused to talk about him. On a few occasions, he opened up to Earl.

"Kevin has problems," he said. "He and Mother don't get along. They haven't ever since Father died. I think Mother blames him for Father's death."

"I would like to meet Kevin. I'm going to marry your mother. I think it's important that I get to know both her sons."

"No, you must not ever go in that basement. Mother would not be happy. That's where Father died. It's a place that no one, other than Kevin, goes."

"But I want to meet your brother, Dennis."

"I'll talk to him, Earl, when the time is right, when Kevin is in a good mood. I can't promise he'll talk to you, but I'll try."

Earl didn't understand. But he didn't want to create problems with his new family. He would go downstairs sometime when Dennis and Jane were not home. He felt compelled to meet Kevin. If he had problems, it was important to realize what the issues were before he married Jane. At some point, he and Kevin's paths were bound to cross.

A week later, the opportunity to go downstairs presented itself. Jane went to the grocery store and Dennis was at the park. Earl was alone in the house. He thought it would be a good time to talk to his future stepson.

The door leading to the basement was unlocked. He opened it and yelled down. "Kevin, are you down there? I'd like to talk to you."

There was no response. He was certain Kevin was down there. He had heard sounds coming from the basement only a few minutes earlier, so he started down the stairs. It was dark. There was no light switch on the wall, so he left the basement door open to provide enough light to maneuver safely down the stairs. At the bottom of the stairs was a single light bulb attached to the basement ceiling. He pulled a chain dangling down from the bulb and the light turned on. The old, dim bulb provided little light, but it was better than nothing at all.

Earl found the basement a bit earie. It reeked of the smell of the chemicals used in the taxidermy process, a smell similar to a combination of bleach and ammonia. The basement was dark and cold. Kevin's completed projects lined the shelves and wall along one side of the basement, birds mainly, some squirrels and other small creatures. They all looked so real— some looked as good in death as they had in life. But there was something disturbing about all of Kevin's projects.

Earl would tell Jane later. "Every animal down there looks angry, like they are ready to attack. Like they know they are trapped and must fight to survive."

The basement seemed even more frightening given the

poor lighting, clutter, and complete quiet. The only sound in the basement was Earl's breathing and his footsteps.

"Kevin, are you down here?" Earl shouted.

There was no response.

Damn, I wish I'd brought a flashlight, he thought.

The only light in the basement came from the eighty-watt lightbulb at the bottom of the basement stairs. There were several windows in the basement that should let in outside light, but they were covered with dark curtains. The light from the single light bulb only illuminated a small portion of the basement. The farther Earl moved inside, the darker it got.

He stopped several times, convinced that someone was watching him. He thought he saw a shadow not far away from him. But when he looked, the shadow disappeared.

No wonder Jane doesn't come down here, he said to himself.

He walked a few more steps and his face collided with a spider web. Earl brushed it off his face with both hands. That's when he heard the door close. Not the door to the basement. It was another door, farther into the basement.

Earl thought about going back. He wanted to go back. His common sense told him to go back.

"Is that you, Jane? Dennis?"

There was no response. He thought about his next move. It was pitch dark where he was in the basement. The only light he could see was behind him, near the stairs where the single light bulb was.

The windows, he thought. *I'll pull the curtain back from the windows.*

He followed the light behind him to one wall of the basement, where he could see a single ray of light beaming to the basement floor. Earl moved slowly toward the light. Just before he reached the window, he heard footsteps behind him. He turned to see a shadow moving quickly a few feet away from him. He could briefly make out the outline of a person within the shadow, then the light went dark — the light bulb turned off. The shadow could no longer be seen. He heard footsteps on the stairs, followed by the basement door closing.

Earl was standing in complete darkness, his heart pounding. Chills were shooting through his body. He moved his body a couple of feet toward the wall and thrust his arms wildly toward the area where he thought the window was, hoping to touch the curtain covering the window.

It is only a few feet away, he thought.

Then he stopped, took a deep breath to calm himself, and remembered the small dot of light he had seen earlier. It was the size of a pen head. He followed the floor with his eyes to the wall.

There it is, he said to himself. A small dot of light at the base of the basement wall.

He moved toward it with his hands stretched out in front of him so he wouldn't bump in to anything. When his hands touched the curtain, he grabbed hold of one edge of it and pulled it down.

It was cloudy and raining outside. There wasn't much light, but it was enough to find his way to the base of the stairs. When he reached them, he pulled the cord dangling down from the light. It turned on. Earl took a deep breath and smiled. It was a great feeling to be able to see again.

Earl hurried up the basement stairs, anxious to get out

of the basement. He turned the knob, opened the door, and saw the person standing in front of him. His heart dropped. His body shook. He lost his balance and started to fall backwards. A hand reached out and grabbed him, pulling him back to safety.

"I'm sorry, Earl. I didn't mean to scare you,"

"Damn, Dennis. I wasn't expecting you to be at the door. You almost caused me to piss my pants. What are you doing there?"

"Mother's back. She wanted me to tell you that dinner will be ready in about thirty-minutes. What are you doing downstairs, Earl? You shouldn't go down in the basement. You promised me you wouldn't. Mother wouldn't want you to."

"I thought I heard a noise down there. I decided to check."

"Did you see anything?"

"No. I thought your brother, Kevin might be down there, but I didn't see him."

"He is down there. Kevin doesn't want anyone but me to go down there. He was hiding from you."

"Are you sure he's all right, Dennis?"

"Yes, he's all right. He just likes to be left alone."

That night, in bed, Earl tried to ask Jane about Kevin. "Jane, you know I love you, and I'm trying my best to get to know your family. But I haven't even met Kevin. He's always in the basement. Granted, I'm not used to teenagers, but don't you find it odd he never comes upstairs?"

"Earl, Kevin has some problems. Life for him has been very difficult. He blames me for most of the troubles in his

life. I really don't want to talk about it. I try my best to forget
he even exists. He's got a dark side to him that scares me. But
as long as we leave him alone, he'll leave us alone. Trust me,
you don't want him coming up from the basement."

"That's crazy, Jane. He's your son. If he has problems,
we need to get him help."

"I told you I don't want to talk about it, Earl. Just leave
him alone. Someday he'll be gone and out of our lives forever.
Please promise me that you'll forget about Kevin, and that
you'll never go into that basement again."

That was the first time it dawned on Earl that he really
didn't know Jane. She was beautiful. That's what had attracted
him to her. But she sure as hell had a lot of baggage. Her boys
were troubled.

The way she talked about Kevin just didn't make any sense,
he thought to himself. *It's just not normal for a boy to hide away
in the basement all the time, and it's not normal for a mother to not
feel some empathy for her own child. Does he go to school?* Earl
wondered. *He must go to school.*

Yet, since moving into the house, Earl had never seen
Kevin leave for school or come home. Dennis did. He saw
Dennis leave and come back from school nearly every day.

There is something very odd about Kevin, Earl thought.

For days after his trip into the basement, Earl couldn't
get Kevin off his mind. He tried to ask Jane questions about
Kevin a few times, but she got angry and refused to talk about
him. Nearly every day he watched Dennis take food down to
the basement for Kevin. He watched as Dennis opened the
basement door, shut it, and locked it from the inside. Earl
tried opening the basement door several times when neither

Dennis or Jane were around. The door was always locked. When Dennis went into the basement at night, Earl could hear two people talking. Their voices were muffled and he couldn't make out the conversation.

As his planned wedding date with Jane neared, Earl felt compelled to have a conversation with Kevin.

"For God's sake," he said to Jane a few days before their wedding date. "I haven't even met Kevin. I've got to at least introduce myself before I marry his mother."

"No," Jane screamed back at him. "He doesn't want to meet you, and I don't want you to meet him. Leave him alone, Earl. Leave him in the basement where he belongs."

Earl dropped the subject. He rarely saw Jane angry, but even the mention of Kevin seemed to send her into a frenzy.

That night, Earl struggled to fall asleep. Jane never had any problem sleeping, mainly because of the sleeping pill she took every night. She slept soundly while Earl tossed and turned that night. No matter what position he tried, he could not get comfortable. His mind kept racing. He was thinking of Kevin and the conversation he'd had with Jane.

She was not being honest with me, he thought. *There is something about Kevin that frightens her. There is something about him that she knows but refuses to tell me.*

He tried to get his mind off Kevin. He tried to think about happier things. But he couldn't.

Finally, about three, he dozed off to sleep. He hadn't gotten into his deep sleep yet when he was awakened by a loud noise in the basement. It sounded like something large had fallen, maybe a shelf. He sat up and looked at Jane. She was sound asleep.

Her sleeping pill must be working, he thought.

He got out of bed and went into the hall. Dennis's bedroom door was closed.

The noise must not have awakened him either, Earl thought.

He walked into the kitchen, grabbed a glass from the cabinet, filled it with water, and took a drink. That's when he heard another loud crash in the basement, this one louder than the first.

He put his glass of water down, walked to the basement door, and turned the handle. It was unlocked.

Earl needed to know what caused the two loud noises. *Maybe Kevin is hurt,* he thought, trying to justify going down to the basement.

After convincing himself it was a good idea to check on him, and that even his mother would agree that, given the two loud crashes, he was justified in checking on her son's well-being, Earl opened the basement door.

"Are you okay, Kevin?" he yelled downstairs.

There was no answer.

He left the basement door open so the light from the kitchen would guide his way safely down the steep and narrow basement stairs. Four steps down, the door suddenly closed behind him. It was pitch black in the basement. He started to turn around to go back up the steps when he felt a hand on his arm. The hand pulled at him, trying to drag him down. He tried to push the hand away when another hand grabbed his ankle and pulled.

Earl struggled to keep his balance. It was a struggle he didn't win. He went tumbling down the basement stairs.

CHAPTER 8
EARL IN THE BASEMENT

The impact of hitting the floor, head first, dazed him. Earl was barely conscious as his body was dragged from the stairs to the room where the cages were housed. He didn't feel his keys and wallet being lifted from his pocket. He had no strength to resist being placed in the cage. His leg and arm were in excruciating pain. Earl slipped between consciousness and unconsciousness.

"I think you broke your leg in the fall, possibly your left arm too. Here's some pain medicine that will help until I'm able to fix them," Dennis told him just before turning out the light and locking the door.

Was I imagining Dennis? he thought. It was possible he was hallucinating.

It was also possible he was imagining what he saw around him. It appeared that he was inside some sort of wire cage. Earl reached his hand out and touched the wires. He pushed, but they had no give. His pain was tremendous, and he couldn't move his left arm and leg.

Earl felt like he was going to pass out again. He lifted the two pills into his mouth and swallowed. Minutes later, he blacked out.

Dennis went into his mother's bedroom — she was still sound asleep. Quietly, so as not to wake Mother, he removed all of Earl's clothes and incidentals from the bathroom. Then he loaded them in Earl's car and went back inside to talk to his brother.

"Why did you push him down the stairs, Kevin?"

"He was too curious about the basement, Dennis. Sooner or later, he would have found the room and seen our special projects. We couldn't let that happen."

"But Mother loves him, Kevin. They were going to be married in less than two weeks. She is going to be very upset."

"Fuck Mother. Boyfriends come a dime a dozen to her. She'll just go in the bar and find another loser to bring home."

"But I think Earl was different from the others. I think he loved her, and I know she loved him. I think he would have been a good father to us."

"Jesus Christ, you naïve son of a bitch. This is why you have me to protect you. Our mother is incapable of finding a good man. She has always been attracted to losers, and she always will. Earl is no different than all the others. We just took care of the problem before his true nature showed its ugliness. If your mother really loved you, she would give up men altogether and concentrate on taking care of you. Every man that has ever been in her life has hurt her and hurt you. Trust me, Earl was no different than the others. He's where he belongs, in a cage in the basement. You take care of him,

Dennis. He's going to make a nice addition to our collection downstairs."

"What about Mother, Kevin? How are we going to explain Earl's disappearance?"

"We're not. He simply left her. When she wakes up, his clothes will be gone, his car will be gone. She will assume he left her. It won't be the first time one of her boyfriends walked out on her."

"She going to be devastated," Dennis said.

"Well you should enjoy that, Dennis. She'll need you again for a few weeks. She'll need you to comfort her, take care of her, and listen to her bullshit until she decides to go out hunting for her next boyfriend. You're going to feel needed for a little while, bro. Now, give me his fucking car keys."

Kevin grabbed the keys from Dennis's hand, left the house, and drove Earl's car away to a place in the woods where he hoped it would not be found.

When Mother woke up three hours later, she looked for Earl in the house.

"I don't know where he is, Mother," Dennis said when she asked him about Earl. "I didn't see him when I got up this morning."

First, she noticed his car was gone.

He probably went to get some coffee, maybe breakfast. Or maybe he needed to run an errand," she thought. *But he always told me where he was going and would kiss me goodbye. Maybe he did and I was sound asleep, and just don't remember it.*

Jane tried calling Earl on his cell phone. There was no answer.

She went to the bedroom and opened the closet. His

clothes were gone. So was his suitcase.

"Dennis," she screamed.

He came running into her bedroom, where he found her on the bed crying.

"What's the matter, Mother."

Dennis knew what the matter was, but he couldn't understand his mother's words. Her cries were drowning out her words. She was shaking. Tears were flowing down her face.

Dennis reached for a tissue and handed it to her, but she just threw it down. He reached for several more and began trying to dry her eyes and face. It was no use. He had never seen his mother that upset before, not even when Father died. He held her tightly, waiting for her to settle down enough to tell him what he already knew. Earl was gone.

Kevin was right. Earl's unexpected departure made Dennis needed again. He felt loved again. For a while Dennis would be the most important, most loved person in his mother's life. She needed him now, and she would for some time. He would nurse her through her grief. He felt special again.

Jane had no idea that the love of her life was just twelve feet below her in a soundproof room.

Dennis didn't like Earl being downstairs. He was fearful his mother might hear him, or that he might escape, or that someone would come looking for him. Dennis worried a lot—always had. That's why Kevin took control of everything that was done in the basement. He was not fearful and did not make mistakes. Kevin was the smarter of the two brothers. He would keep Dennis safe.

Dennis trusted his brother and did exactly what Kevin told him to do. He knew that as long as he did what Kevin instructed him to do, everything would turn out all right.

So, when Kevin instructed Dennis to keep mother medicated, he did exactly as he was told.

"She is suffering now," Kevin said. "Give her the medication every four hours. That will keep her asleep. She can rest and keep her mind off Earl until we are done with him."

When Mother was sound asleep, Dennis went down to the basement to tend to Earl's injuries. His brother had instructed him to take care of their guest, to nurse him back to health. He didn't understand why, because he knew what his brother had planned for Earl, but he did as his brother instructed.

As soon as he opened the door to the soundproof room, Earl began screaming. Kevin had told him that would happen. He shut and locked the door behind him. Earl's screams hurt Dennis's ears and gave him a headache, but he knew the screams could not be heard outside of that room. Kevin had done a wonderful job insulating the room from noise escaping.

"Earl, I want to help you. I know you are in pain. I've got some medicine that will make you feel better, and I've brought you a sandwich. Please calm down and I'll open the cage and help you."

"You're fucking crazy. Get me out of here and I won't tell the police."

"I wish I could, but Kevin told me you need to stay in the cage for a while."

"You've lost your mind, and so has your brother. Where the hell is he?"

"He's in the basement."

"Call him in here. I want to talk to both of you. You're going to be in some serious trouble if you don't let me go right away. You pushed me down the stairs. You broke my leg and arm, and you're holding me in a cage. Do you have any idea what the police are going to do to you when they find out? And what about your mother? Does she have any idea what you have done to me?"

"Leave Mother out of this. She has no idea you are down here. She thinks you ran off. She is heartbroken. She really did love you."

"Why are you doing this, Dennis?"

"I didn't do it, Earl. Kevin did. He pushed you down the stairs. He put you in the cage. I'm sorry he did it, but I'm sure he had a good reason."

"Let me talk to him, Dennis. I'm sure we can work out whatever problem he has with me."

"I'm afraid that wouldn't do any good. Kevin doesn't want to talk to you until he is ready. Besides, he won't change his mind. Kevin never changes his mind. You'll just need to wait until he is ready for you. Until them, he has instructed me to take good care of you. I'm to make you as comfortable as possible. I will make sure that you are warm, get plenty of food to eat, and water to drink. I will provide you pain medication to help until your leg and arm heal."

"My arm and leg are broken, Dennis. I need a doctor. I should be in the hospital."

"I'm afraid Kevin won't allow that to happen. But

I think I can help. I've had some experience setting broken bones. But first you need to take the pain medicine. You're going to need it."

Dennis unlocked the cage and sat a peanut butter and jelly sandwich down next to Earl, along with a cold glass of water. "You should eat this after I give you the medicine. It will put you to sleep in about ten minutes, so you better eat right away." He placed the pill in his right hand and held the glass of water in his left. "Open up," he said.

When Earl opened his mouth, he placed the pill on his tongue.

"Drink this. You'll feel a lot better in a few minutes."

After swallowing the pill, Earl looked at Dennis and said, "You're not like your brother, Dennis. I can tell. You're gentle and caring, just like your mother. You wouldn't hurt me. I know that. But your brother would. God only knows what he has planned for me. Don't let him do it, Dennis. Your mother and I can get him help. You, me, and your mother can still be a family. You need a father. Your mother needs a husband. I want to take care of both of you. Just let me out of here and we can be a family. Or, if you're afraid of your brother, tell your mother where I am. She'll do the right thing."

"You better eat your sandwich, Earl. I'll check on you later."

Dennis walked out of the room, locking the door behind him. Kevin was waiting for him.

"How's his leg and arm, Dennis? Can you fix them?"

"I don't know. They are in bad shape—compound fractures, I believe. The bone in his leg has broken through the skin. It's swollen and purple in color. I don't know if I can fix it. The arm is not as bad. I think I can reset it."

"Do your best, Dennis. You better go to the drug store and get whatever you need. Mother will have some money in her purse."

Dennis went into his mother's bedroom. She was sound asleep.

The medication works very well, he thought.

He located his mother's purse on her dresser, opened it, and removed the cash. *Only $32,* he said to himself. *That won't be enough.*

He reached inside for her bank card, took it out, and put it in his pocket. He would stop at the ATM on the way.

Dennis bought a splint and bandages to fix Earl's arm. Then he drove to the hardware store. There he bought a bone saw. Earl's leg was too far gone to put in a splint.

He returned home and made lunch for himself. He didn't make it for his mother or Earl—they would still be sound asleep. He wouldn't need to feed them for a while. After lunch, exactly four hours after he'd given her the last pill, he went into his mother's room, lifted her head, opened her mouth, and put a pill inside. Then he poured water into her mouth and forced the pill down her throat. Satisfied she had swallowed the pill, he kissed his mother on the cheek, laid her head back on the pillow, and walked out of the room.

He carried the supplies he picked up from the drug store down to the basement. After forcing another sleeping pill into Earl's mouth, he began his work to repair his arm and leg. He worked on the arm first. That was the easy part. The bone is his forearm was protruding slightly above the skin but had not broken the surface. There was some bruising and discoloration of the skin, but nothing too serious. Dennis grabbed Earl's hand just above the wrist with both his hands, tightened his grip, and pulled with all his strength. He heard a popping sound and saw the bump in his skin surface disappear.

"The pain must have been tremendous," Dennis told Kevin later. "But the sleeping pills worked. Earl didn't wake up."

With the bone back in place, or close anyway, Dennis cut two splints to fit the length of Earl's forearm. He placed one on top of the forearm and the other underneath, and wrapped the two tightly together with masking tape.

Dennis couldn't help but smile at his handiwork. *A doctor couldn't have done much better,* he thought to himself.

The arm was the easy part. Dennis did not look forward to what he needed to do next.

Earl had slept through the repairs on his arm, but Dennis wasn't sure he would sleep through the work on his leg. He couldn't imagine anyone sleeping through the type of pain he was about to endure.

He picked up three more sleeping pills and a glass of water, opened Earl's mouth slightly, placed the pills on his tongue, lifted his head, and poured the water in his mouth. Dennis watched as the pills slid down his throat. He guessed it would take about thirty minutes for the pills to take effect. Dennis used that time to move Earl to a workbench at the other end of the room. He dragged him twenty feet to the workbench, but struggled to lift him onto the table. His sedated body weighed more than Dennis thought it would. Dennis tied a rope around Earl's waist and another one around his chest, and used the other end of the rope like a pulley, slowly lifting him onto the workbench. When he had Earl positioned on the table where he wanted him, Dennis used the ropes to tie him securely to the table. Dennis was fearful that Earl would wake up during the process. The rope would keep him secure.

After allowing enough time for the medication to take hold, Dennis cut and removed the pants leg from the area he needed to work. Then he took a container of alcohol and generously applied it to the leg. He picked up the bone saw and began to saw in the area just above the discolored section of the leg. As the blade cut into flesh, blood splattered on Dennis's face and hands. The sight of skin parting to reveal bone sickened his stomach. He stopped three different times to throw-up.

Kevin has the stomach for this, not me, he told himself.

But taking care of projects wasn't Kevin's job. It was his. He knew that. Kevin was the artist. He was the caretaker.

Cutting through the skin, the flesh, the fatty substance underneath was the easy part. Cutting through bone was difficult. It took all his strength to saw through it. It was a slow, difficult process. The sound the saw made cutting through dense bone was unlike anything he had ever heard before, and was a sound that he would never forget. Dennis had sawed through the base of a dead oak tree before. This was nothing like that. A human leg bone was more solid, more dense than a dead oak tree. It spit tiny bone fragments back into Dennis's face as he sawed through it.

After removing the lower portion of Earl's leg, Dennis took skin and muscle flap from the damaged leg and sewed it to the stump. Earl didn't wake up throughout the amputation.

Body tissue, blood, and pieces of bone coated Dennis's shirt, pants, and face by the time he had finished. There was considerable clean-up to do. Dennis dragged Earl back to his cage, covered him with blankets, and proceeded to clean up the mess.

"Geez, Dennis. You look like crap," Kevin said with a smile on his face when Dennis exited the room.

"Please don't make me do that again. I'm going to need to throw these clothes away so Mother doesn't see them. Kevin, I don't understand why you had me cut off his leg when you will be done with him in a few days."

"Dennis, that's why I give the orders and you follow them. I only work on healthy specimens. I can't do them justice if they are damaged before I work on them. Besides, I've never worked on a one-legged project before. This will challenge me."

Dennis went upstairs, showered, changed clothes, and wrapped his work clothes in plastic. When he was dressed, he took the plastic bag outside and placed it in the large, metal trash container, with the remainder of Earl's damaged leg and towels he'd used to clean up the basement.

The garbage man will pick up tomorrow, he said to himself.

Dennis ate like it was his last meal that night. The work in the basement had given him quite an appetite. Spaghetti and meatballs — Mother's recipe — garlic toast, and candied carrots. He took a tray into his mother's room. She was still sleeping. The drugs he had given her were potent. He sat the food tray on the nightstand next to the bed. Then he gently touched his mother's shoulder.

"Mother, dinner is ready."

She did not move. He shook her body gently.

"Mother, it's time to wake up. You need to eat something."

Slowly, she began to open one eye and then the other. "I don't feel like eating," she said in a low whisper.

"Mother, if you don't eat something, I'm going to need to feed you myself. Besides, I made your favorite, spaghetti and meatballs, just the way you like it."

Dennis helped her sit up and then moved the tray to her lap. He took a napkin from the tray and tucked it on her lap.

"Drink a sip of water first," he said, picking up the glass and tilting it toward her mouth. She drank three sips and motioned for Dennis to take the glass away.

He put the glass down and scooped up a fork full of noodles and a small piece of meatball. "Take a taste, Mother. I think I did a very good job on this meal. I followed your recipe."

After a half dozen bites, Mother motioned for Dennis to take the tray away.

"You really need to eat more, Mother. You're going to waste away eating like a bird." Dennis picked up the tray, gave his mother a kiss on the cheek, and started out the door.

"Dennis, have you heard from Earl?"

"No, Mother."

"If you do, promise me that you'll let me know as soon as you hear something."

"I will."

"And Dennis, please don't give me any more sleeping

pills. I think I've slept enough."

"Yes, Mother."

Dennis decided not to tell her it was too late. He'd crushed up several pills and mixed them in her water and spaghetti sauce. She would be sound asleep in less than thirty minutes.

He was washing the dishes from that night's meal when he heard the noise in the basement. Dennis stopped what he was doing and ran downstairs. The noise was coming from the room where Earl was kept. The room was soundproof, so it took quite a racket for noise to escape that room. He hurried to the door, unlocked it, and heard the screams of a man that just discovered his leg was gone.

Dennis had forgotten to medicate Earl when he put him back in the cage after removing his leg. He was in excruciating pain, and the shock of seeing that his leg was gone added to his hysteria. Dennis closed the door behind him so as not to let the screams escape the room more than they already were.

"Fuck you, Dennis. What happen to my fucking leg? What the hell have you and your sick brother done?"

"Please, Earl, calm down. I've got pain medication that will make you feel a lot better. Just settle down so I can give it to you."

"Fuck you, Dennis. You open this cage and I'll rip your head apart, you sadistic son of a bitch."

"You don't mean it, Earl. You love my mother. You know she's not a bitch."

"If you come near me, you little bastard, I'm going to kill you."

"Earl, if you don't settle down, I'm going to need to get

Kevin, and I really don't think you want him coming in here. He has a very bad temper."

"Get your fucking brother. I want to talk to him. But first, toss the pain medicine in the cage."

Dennis reached between the bars of the cage and dropped a container of three white pills inside. Earl grabbed them and swallowed in one swift movement.

"Now get your fucking brother."

Dennis turned and walked out of the room.

"Kevin, he wants to talk to you," Dennis said.

Five minutes later, the door to the room opened and Kevin walked in, closing the door behind him.

"My brother said you insist on talking to me. What the hell do you want, Earl?"

"Kevin?" he asked. "What the fuck?"

CHAPTER 9
KEVIN GOES HOME

Earl stayed in the basement for seven days before Kevin used his creative skills and made him a permanent resident of the basement.

Mother did not get over her grief of losing Earl like Kevin had predicted. She was never the same after Earl disappeared from her life. Jane never dated again. She sank into depression and never left the house. Hell, she rarely came out of the bedroom. Dennis spent hours each day in her room, watching television with her, feeding her, helping her change her clothes, shower, and use the bathroom. Jane rarely uttered a word, staring blankly in front of her most of the time.

"She needs a psychiatrist," Kevin said.

"No, I can take care of her," Dennis replied.

She needed Dennis more than ever, and he enjoyed being needed.

The loss of Earl had sent Jane's mind spiraling into complete darkness. She could no longer function by herself.

Her bedroom became her prison, and Dennis became her only bridge between sanity and insanity.

Dennis loved his mother, more now than ever before. She was completely dependent on him. He didn't need to worry about some other man entering her life and occupying her time. She wasn't going anywhere now. Her nights in Kelly's bar were over. Her mind might have been saved if Dennis chose to get her help. But he was too selfish to do that. He liked his mother in the state she was in, needy and completely dependent on him.

Dennis and Kevin drifted apart for a while after Earl became a trophy in the basement. Dennis blamed his brother for his mother's depression. He was the one that pushed Earl down the basement stairs and was the one responsible for Earl's disappearance. Kevin had caused their mother's grief.

For the first time in his life, Dennis was disappointed in his brother. For over a year, Dennis only went into the basement to dust off the finished projects, the trophies of Kevin's artistry. Earl was Kevin's final project for over a year. The cages went empty. The work bench, unused.

Dennis still left the back door unlocked for his brother to come and go as he pleased, but he never saw Kevin enter or leave the house. He heard noises in the basement from time-to-time, normally in the middle of the night.

There were numerous times when Dennis was in the basement or went down to investigate a noise that he saw shadow on the walls and floor of the basement. He would call out his brother's name. But there was no response.

If Kevin is down here, he doesn't want to be seen, Dennis thought.

Without Kevin around, the basement was a lonely, spooky place for Dennis. He didn't like being down there, but he had a responsibility to care for its residents. They needed to be cleaned, they needed to be moved around. They needed to socialize with other residents of the basement. They needed someone to talk to them. That was Dennis's job.

Besides, he knew Kevin was watching him. He knew Kevin would be upset if he didn't take care of his finished projects. Even though he didn't see Kevin, the shadows told him he was there in the basement, watching.

***

Kevin became a talented embalmer over the years at Malott Funeral Home. His skills in the basement carried over to his work on the embalming table. The job was a perfect fit for him. Kevin was not a social person. He was awkward around others, and people, in general, were put off by his lack of a personality. Mike Malott recognized Kevin's shortcomings. He didn't allow him to talk to families or require him to socialize with other employees. He gave him only one job, embalming.

Inside the cold, isolated embalming room in the basement of the funeral home, Kevin was comfortable. Kevin was free to be an artist. That was his home away from home.

When a body came in, the funeral home notified Kevin, and he would come into the basement of the funeral home and apply his skill to the deceased. He was a true artist. No matter what state the deceased arrived in, he could make them look as good or better than they had in life. Gunshots to the face, fire victims, facial disfigurements, drowning victims that had been in the water for long periods of time, were beyond most embalmer's capabilities, and would require a closed casket. But not for Kevin. His skills were better than the others. He could take almost any corpse, regardless of the damage, and make it look like they had never been through a trauma.

Mike Malott recognized his skills and rewarded him with the freedom, flexibility, and privacy Kevin's artistic skills required.

He built a private entrance into the embalming room from the outside so Kevin could come and go as he pleased. He provided him a private cell phone that was used to contact him when a body arrived in his embalming room. Communication was done through text messages. When Kevin was done preparing a body, he would text a message to Mike Malott.

After the first year he was employed at the funeral home, Kevin was never seen by another member of the staff. All communication was done through text messages. Kevin's paychecks were mailed to a P.O. box.

Mike Malott had never gone to such lengths to keep an employee happy before. It was the oddest situation he had ever encountered. But Kevin was worth it. He was truly an artist. Families were pleased with his artistry. Their loved one had never looked better, they often said. During the entire time Kevin was their embalmer, there was never one family member that complained about how their loved one looked. The reputation of Malott Funeral Home was greatly improved because of the magic Kevin performed on that embalming table.

His flexible work hours gave Kevin time to try to repair his marriage. Since Dennis and he had drifted apart, he had no one else in his life. Kevin wouldn't admit it, but he was lonely. He needed someone, anyone to care about him. Kevin was tough on the outside but weak on the inside. He pushed people away, but secretly wanted them to stay.

For several months, he had stayed in the basement of his mother's house. Kevin had not been home and had not talked to his wife or his stepdaughters. He had thought he didn't need them anymore. Kevin was right as long as he had Dennis in his life. But now that his brother refused to acknowledge him, he needed someone.

For days he watched his house, wondering if he would be welcomed, wondering if Marsha still wanted him in her life, wondering if his stepdaughters cared anymore. He had tried to go inside the first day, when he had seen his wife and stepdaughters leave and was certain no one was in the house. The door was locked. He tried his key. It did not work,

Marsha changed the locks, he thought to himself.

He went to the rear door. It was locked too, and the lock had been changed. He tried several windows, but they were all locked. So he decided to watch and wait.

That first evening, he watched as a black Pontiac Trans Am pulled into the driveway. The horn blasted two times. A few seconds later, Marsha came out of the house, wearing a red halter top, jean shorts cut so short they barely covered her ass, cowboy boots, and a cowboy hat. She got into the passenger side of the car, gave a long, passionate kiss to the driver, a man that appeared to be much younger than she was, and they drove away. Kevin followed them.

She needed men, lots of men. They made her feel attractive, they made her feel wanted. Kevin understood that.

He wasn't jealous. God knows he had plenty of reason to be, but he wasn't. He'd accepted that she would have other men in her life before they got married. But he had always hoped that he would be the most important one.

Their marriage was not a traditional one. They didn't love each other. Instead, they were dependent on each other. They were crutches to each other's depravities. They came to each other when there was no one else to turn to, during the lowest points of their life.

The problem was that their lowest points rarely occurred at the same time.

Kevin was at his lowest point now. Marsha was not. He needed to do something about that.

He watched as the black Trans Am pulled into the parking lot of Billy Bob's, a country music bar on the outskirts of town. Kevin parked a row away from where the Trans Am was parked. He watched as a young man, thinly built, wearing a large good necklace around his neck, and with long hair that fell below his shoulders, walked hand-in-hand with Marsha into the bar. Her boyfriend appeared ten-years younger than his wife.

Billy Bob's was a huge country music bar, occupying what appeared to be an old abandoned warehouse. The parking lot covered a city block and was about two-thirds full. Kevin waited about ten-minutes and then entered the bar. In the center was a large dance floor that was about the size of half a football field. A band played on an elevated platform at one corner of the dance floor.

Two large bars spanning fifty feet, both containing three dozen varieties of whiskey and fifteen varieties of draft beer, occupied opposite sides of Billy Bob's. Tables, hundreds of them it appeared, occupied the open space between the dance floor and bars. The place was packed with people of all ages, nearly all white, most wearing cowboy boots and hats. Most were urban cowboys — pretend cowboys.

Kevin scanned the area around him looking for his wife. When he didn't see her, he moved slowly toward another section and scanned the area again. He found her sitting on a bar stool at the large bar on the north side of the room, her friend seated next to her. The young man had long, straight brown hair that stretched past his shoulders and down several inches of his back. His hair looked like thin spaghetti noodles flowing loosely and ungroomed. His oversized dark brown cowboy hat shaded his face and covered much of his thinning hair. He wore tight jeans that molded to his skin.

He was exactly the type of man his wife had been attracted to in the past. Kevin watched as they danced, close and slow. He watched as they kissed and fondled each other. Kevin wasn't upset. He didn't feel jealousy. Her dime store cowboy boyfriend was just an obstacle to Kevin getting what he needed right now.

Kevin sat at a table thirty feet away, nursed a few beers, but not of enough frequency or quantity to intoxicate him. He studied the two of them. Her husband wanted to believe the cowboy was of little interest to his wife, that he was just another man to keep her warm at night and make her feel attractive. But the look in her eyes, the smile on her face, her laughter all told him something else. She was falling in love with him.

The look in cowboy's eyes did not return the feelings.

Kevin watched as the cowboy's eyes wandered to other, younger, more attractive women in the bar. Marsha was past her prime now. No amount of make-up, no tight-fitting dress or braless tube top, could hide her fading beauty. Her tits were perking, but not firm. They drooped just a little. Her belly was not as firm as it used to be. Her ass was not as alluring. She was attractive, but she was on the decline.

The cowboy wants her now, but that isn't going to last, Kevin thought.

He felt sorry for his wife. Her looks were everything to her. She had to feel wanted. Marsha had always fed off the looks men gave her, prided herself on being able to have any man she wanted. His wife was always the hunted, never the hunter. But those days were slipping away. Age was catching up to her.

She has to see his wandering eyes, Kevin told himself. *She must know he is only using her.*

But if she did, his wife appeared to be ignoring it. Kevin wasn't ignoring it. Kevin wasn't going to let his wife get hurt again.

Their marriage had always been unconventional. They both cared for each other. It wasn't love, but it wasn't friendship either. The two of them were dependent on each other even though there were many times they couldn't stand each other. There were times they wanted to kill each other. They lived apart for long periods of time. Both carried on separate lives that merged together only at the lowest points in their lives, only when they had no one else to turn to.

The band sang their last song a few minutes before two. Shortly after, the last remaining customers began exiting the bar, Marsha and her cowboy among them. They staggered out of the bar and to their car, stopping next to it for a long, passionate kiss, then got inside and drove away. Kevin followed them back to his house and watched as they went inside. Kevin followed the lights in the house as they turned on from the living room up to the bedroom. He watched the window to the master bedroom. The shade was up. The curtains were open.

Kevin watched as the cowboy undressed Marsha. Then she undressed him. He watched as the cowboy kissed her tenderly on the lips and moved his tongue slowly down her body, stopping at her tits to massage them with his tongue, slowly circling her breasts with his tongue next to her nipples, but careful not to touch them. Kevin watched as his wife's eyes rolled back with pleasure. Her husband watched as the cowboy moved his tongue to her nipples. He saw Marsha grab hold of the back of her lover's head and pull it closer to her, begging him to tighten his hold on her nipples. Then he saw her fall to the bed. The view from his car would not allow him to see her lying on the bed. The last thing he saw was her lover pulling out a pair of handcuffs and going down on the bed with her.

Kevin knew exactly what was going on. He had played the same role as her lover before. His wife likes rough sex. She liked bondage and enjoyed being handcuffed and tied down so she had no control.

Watching his wife get pleasure from another man excited Kevin. He had a raging hard-on. Kevin unzipped his pants and pulled it out, and began to stroke it.

Then he heard the scream coming from the bedroom.

He saw the blood splatter upward from the bed onto the wall. Kevin saw the baseball bat raised high in the air and falling down quickly, causing another splatter of blood, another scream, more desperate than the last. The bat raised again and was thrust downward — more blood, but no more screams.

A light from the girls' room came on.

Their mother's screams must have woken them, Kevin thought.

Christina was the first to rush to her mother's bedroom. She opened the door to see the cowboy standing over the blood-soaked body of her mother. She ran from the room. The cowboy, naked and bloodied, ran after her. He swung the bat, catching the edge of her lower back, the force knocking her to the ground. That's when Melinda came out of her room, just ten-feet away.

"Run, Melinda," Christina yelled.

The cowboy turned around to see the other sister. He swung the bat toward her, clipping her elbow. She ran toward the bathroom. He turned his attention back to Christina, lifting the bat high in the air. She laid on the ground, motionless with fear. Christina closed her eyes, preparing for the next blow. That's when she heard the gunshot — one shot, two shots, and finally a third. The cowboy dropped the bat and fell forward onto Christina.

"It's okay, Christina," Kevin said, leaning over her. "He can't hurt you anymore."

The police and three ambulances arrived thirty minutes later. Christina was carried out first. Emotionally, she was a wreck. Physically, she was fine except for a large bruise on her lower back where the bat had struck her. Melinda was taken out next. The bat had shattered her elbow. She would need surgery.

Marsha was dead — so was the cowboy. They left them in the house until the crime scene investigators were done. Kevin was taken to the police station and questioned there by Detective Baczenas.

"Mr. Collins, I understand the grief you are going through right now, but if you feel up to it, I would like to ask you some questions. Is that okay?"

"Yes, Detective."

"I understand from talking to your stepdaughter that you haven't been living in the house for several months. What made you decide to come home tonight?"

"My wife and I have been separated, Detective. We've been trying to work out our differences. I came home tonight in hopes that we could talk. I've missed her and the girls very much, and I thought if I could sit down with Marsha, we could work out our problems, and I could get my family back again. It's been very lonely for me the last few months away from them."

"So did you talk to your wife?"

"No, I didn't. When I arrived home about seven last night, a black Trans Am was parked in the driveway. I decided to sit and wait to see if whoever was visiting the house would leave soon. A few minutes later, my wife came out of the house with a man, holding hands and kissing. I tell you, seeing them together nearly broke my heart. I know I should have left right then, but I couldn't. Something inside of me kept telling me to follow them. So, I did. They went to a country bar on the other side of town. I think the name of the bar was Billy Bob's. I followed them into the bar and watched. I know that sounds crazy, but I needed to know if she was in love with him. I needed to know if there was any hope of us getting back together."

"What did you decide?" Detective Baczenas asked.

"I could tell she was in love with him. But I could also tell he wasn't in love with her. I could tell that by the way he looked at other women when he didn't think she was watching. I could tell he was a player. She was just another one-night stand to him."

"So, did you try to talk to her? Or did you confront him?"

"No, Detective. I just sat there watching them until the bar closed and they left."

"What did you do then?"

"I followed them. I don't know why. I just wanted to know where they were going."

"Where did they go?"

"They went to our house. They went in the front door and up the stairs to the bedroom. I couldn't believe my wife was taking another man to our bed. I was hurt. I was upset."

"Why didn't you leave?"

"I thought about it. Part of me wanted to leave. But something in my gut told me I should stay. There was something about the cowboy's eyes that told me that she wasn't safe with him."

"Your wife was cheating on you, Mr. Collins. I just can't understand why you would want to watch as she took another man into her bed. You must have hated her. You must have wanted her dead."

"No, Detective. I didn't. Marsha had a lot of boyfriends during the time we were married. She couldn't help herself. It was a sickness. She was addicted to sex. I wasn't enough for her—I knew that before we even got married. I accepted her weakness. I didn't like it, but I accepted it because I loved her."

"So, what did you see from outside her window?"

"I saw the lights go on in the bedroom, and saw them kissing. I saw him pull out the handcuffs, then they got on the bed. I couldn't see anything after that. My view only allowed me to see the upper half of the bedroom from the ground. The bed was too low. I didn't have a view of that."

"So, when did you decide to go inside the house?"

"I heard a scream. It was Marsha's voice. Then I saw the man stand up. I saw him raise a baseball bat high above his head and swing it downward toward the bed. I heard more screams, and I saw what looked like blood splatter up from the bed. That's when I ran to the house. The door was locked, so I broke through a window in the living room, climbed inside, and went to the kitchen, where Marsha kept her gun. She was always afraid of being alone, and our neighborhood has had several break-ins over the years. I grabbed the gun and ran upstairs. Then I heard the girls screaming. I saw him standing over Christina with the baseball bat raised. That's when I fired the shots."

"Did you do anything else, Mr. Collins, before you called the police?"

"The man landed on Christina. I pulled him off her and helped her up. I told her everything was okay. Then I checked on Melinda. She was in the bathroom. She was in a lot of pain. That's when I called 911. After calling, I went into the bedroom. Marsha was naked, handcuffed on the bed, covered in blood. Her face was not recognizable. He must have smashed her in the face several times with the bat."

"Mr. Collins, I am curious about something. Why would your wife keep her gun in the kitchen? It seems like an odd place to store a gun."

"I never really thought about it, Detective. Ever since we were married, she has kept the gun in a locked drawer next to the sink."

"But we didn't see any sign of the lock being broken on the drawer. Do you have a key, Mr. Collins?"

"No, it was unlocked."

"Kevin, one more question—have we met before?"

"No, I don't think so, Detective."

"I'm pretty good at remembering faces, and yours seems familiar."

"I don't remember seeing you before, Detective."

"You're probably right, Mr. Collins."

Two days later, after thoroughly interviewing Christina and Melinda, Detective Baczenas closed the case. The death of the cowboy was ruled justifiable homicide.

Marsha's mother, retired for the last seven years, came to make funeral arrangements for her daughter. She refused to let Kevin participate. She didn't even want him to attend the visitation or funeral. He came anyway.

Marsha's mother had always disliked Kevin—she blamed him for her daughter's troubles. She found his character odd and not trustworthy. After burying her daughter, she took Christina and Melinda back to Florida with her. Kevin was only the stepfather. He had no right to keep them with him, which suited him fine. He would not be a good father.

***

There were a couple of things that haunted Detective Baczenas about Kevin Collins.

He never shed a tear for his murdered wife, the detective wrote in his paperwork. *He didn't appear to have any emotion at all.*

The other thing that bothered him was the gun. It was confirmed that the gun was owned by Kevin's wife, but the detective couldn't shake the gut feeling that Kevin didn't get that gun from the drawer in the kitchen. It didn't make sense that, with two teenage girls in the house, their mother would be so careless as to leave a loaded gun in an unlocked drawer in the kitchen. He had asked both her daughters about the gun, and neither knew that their mother had it.

If Kevin didn't get the gun from an unlocked drawer, why would he lie about it? the detective thought to himself.

The gun that Kevin used to kill the cowboy turned out to be registered to Marsha. Fingerprints lifted from the gun were those of Marsha, and Kevin.

The investigation of the cowboy pulled up some interesting facts, too. His name was Michael Clay. He had served five years in prison for armed robbery. He was unemployed as far as Detective Baczenas could determine, had been for over a year, but he had several thousand dollars in his bank account. Most of the money had been deposited within the last three months, in deposits of one-thousand to five-thousand each, all cash.

Michael Clay was up to something. The detective was

convinced of it. But he wasn't sure what it was.

***

Kevin stayed in the house after his wife's murder. He cleaned up the blood from the walls in the bedroom, from the hallway near the stairs, from the bathroom where Melinda hid. He threw out the blood-stained mattress and sheets and replaced the nightstands coated in his wife's blood. Kevin replaced the stained carpet from the bedroom and hallway. He repaired the window he had broken to enter the house, and changed the locks on the doors. But whenever he left the house, he felt the eyes of his neighbors. Kevin had never been liked by his neighbors. But now that a murder had taken place in his house, he was not only disliked, but he was hated by some and feared by most. For sale signs went up throughout the neighborhood. People wanted to move. But the murder had been on all the news channels. It was on the radio. It was in the newspapers. To sell a home in the neighborhood, the price would need to be reduced substantially. Some neighbors, so desperate to move, took losses on their homes to sell them. Others, unwilling or unable to take a loss, stayed. Those were the ones that hated Kevin the most. They were the ones that left hateful messages on his door or in his mail box, or on his garage door. Those were the ones that wanted him dead.

But Kevin had no place to go. Dennis had made it clear that he no longer wanted him in his life. His house was his only sanctuary.

***

Dennis saw the news about the murder of Kevin's wife on television. For a few minutes, he considered reaching out to his brother. But then he thought about what Kevin had made him do to Earl. He thought about the evil inside his brother's soul.

Kevin is incapable of feelings, he told himself. *Bringing him back into my life would only bring more hurt and destruction.*

So. Dennis didn't contact Kevin. For now, he had Mother. She occupied all his time. She was a loving, caring person, not like Kevin. Kevin made him do things he didn't want to do. Kevin was a bad person. Dennis didn't like the dark side of his personality that Kevin forced out of him when they were together.

Besides, Dennis was convinced that the shadows in the basement were his brother, and that his brother was watching him. He was convinced that many times when he went into the basement to care for the finished projects, his brother was watching him. He had left the back door to the house unlocked, as Kevin had instructed him, so his brother could come and go as he pleased.

And, although he didn't see Kevin enter or leave, the moving shadows in the basement convinced him that Kevin was there.

There were times Dennis thought about locking the back door, but those were fleeting thoughts. He was afraid of Kevin, of what Kevin would do to him if he locked that back door. He had given Dennis instructions to always leave the back door unlocked, and Dennis had always done exactly what his brother told him to.

***

Kevin lived a simple life by himself in that house. He went into the funeral home whenever he was called, but that was only a few times a week, normally. During the daylight hours, when he wasn't working, he sat quietly and watched television or listened to music. Kevin made himself a bowl of cereal and coffee for breakfast, a peanut butter and jelly sandwich for lunch, and a TV dinner for supper. He thought a lot about resuming his hobby, but all his tools were at his mother's house, and he refused to go back to get them. At night, he went to Kelly's Tavern. He sat by himself, watched people, and drank Old Crow with a beer chaser. Kevin drank until the bar closed and staggered back to his car to drive home. It was a wonder that he never got pulled over. There were many nights he didn't even remember going home. Drinking made him feel less lonely. It numbed his pain. It dulled his loneliness.

Kevin spent more hours at a table in the corner of Kelly's than he did at home.

He needed some purpose in his life. He needed some reason to live. Kevin found that purpose late one Friday night at Kelly's.

CHAPTER 10
A NEW PURPOSE

It was a little past 1 a.m. Out of the corner of his eye, Kevin saw a man and woman arguing at a pool table on the other side of the bar. Their conversation became heated. The man, older, maybe in his fifties, heavy-set with a large bear belly, towered over his tiny, petite, much younger partner. The woman, in her twenties or early thirties, with long, thick dark hair that flowed down her back to within inches of her waist, reminded Kevin of Marsha. She wasn't particularly attractive, but she dressed to maximize her assets. Her make-up was heavy, her eyeliner thick. Her jeans were tight. The spaghetti strap top she wore fit snugly to her skin and showed most of her breasts. Her nipples showed through the top, pointing slightly downward.

She could be a hooker, Kevin thought.

But he didn't think so. He speculated that she was a divorcee, lonely and looking for someone to make her night a little less lonely.

"You fucking tease," he heard the man yell.

"You're an asshole," she responded. "Leave me alone."

Kevin watched as the man grabbed her arm and began pulling her toward the door. She was screaming at the man as he pulled her closer to the exit door.

"Leave me alone, you fucking asshole."

People in the bar looked but no one came to the woman's rescue. The man pulled her out of the bar and to his pick-up truck. Kevin walked out of the bar a few minutes later. He heard the struggle in the truck and heard the woman's cries. He went to his car, opened the trunk, and pulled out a tire iron. Kevin shut the trunk and walked slowly toward the woman's cries, looking around as he walked to see if anyone was watching.

When he reached the passenger door of the truck, he looked inside. The woman was lying on her back on the bench seat. Her top was pulled up, exposing her tits, and her pants were off, lying on the floor beneath her. The man was on top of her, naked from the waist down, and pounding his meat inside her with all the force he could muster. Her eyes were large and wet. Her make-up was flowing down her cheeks chased by her tears. She looked up to see Kevin looking through the window. Her eyes focused on his, begging him to help.

He tried to open the passenger door. It was locked. But the sound alerted the woman's attacker. He glared back at Kevin.

"Get out of here, you fucking pervert," he yelled.

Kevin backed off and walked out of the man's sight.

"That will teach him," the man said out loud.

The man quickened the pace, feeling that his manhood was ready to explode. He thrust deep inside her and then lifted slowly until he was nearly out of her, then thrust deep inside her again. He felt his juices rushing toward her and was moments away from satisfaction when he heard the shattering of the glass. Pieces of the window fell on his back, some jagged, some penetrating his flesh. Before he could rise off the woman, he felt the sharp edge of the tire iron penetrate his skull. He never got a chance to fight back. Three quick, powerful strikes to the head and he felt no more pain.

The woman, desperate to get free, pushed the man off her, his limp, bloodied body rolling onto the floorboard of his truck. She pulled down her top, grabbed her jeans, and began to pull them up when she glanced out the window. Kevin was gone.

Kevin felt a huge adrenalin rush with each blow of the tire iron. The excitement of that night lasted for several days. But there was one thing missing—he had no trophy to keep his memories of that night alive. The excitement of killing something or someone, particularly someone that deserved it, had always been short-lived. That's why it had always been so important to bring them back to life in that basement.

He could still use that basement, even if his brother didn't want him to. He could resume his work. All the tools of his trade were down there. The door was unlocked—Kevin was certain that Dennis wouldn't go against his wishes and lock it. The tools he had in the basement would bring his projects back to life. They would be lasting memories for him. He could have the best of both worlds. He could have the excitement of seeing the last breath of life drain from a deserving soul, and he could have a permanent trophy to constantly remind him of the thrill of taking a life.

Kevin was excited again. He had a new purpose. Suddenly his life didn't seem meaningless. Suddenly he wasn't lonely and depressed.

Perhaps, with time, my presence back in Mother's basement might help rebuild the relationship between me and Dennis, Kevin thought.

But first, Kevin needed to retrieve his last victim. She needed to occupy a space in the basement. The excitement of those killings had faded. He needed permanent reminders of those nights.

Kevin had kept the newspaper clipping of the murder in the parking lot of Kelly's. The newspaper and television called the killer a vigilante. He liked that term. They said he came to the aid of a rape victim, and made him sound like a hero. It made Kevin feel proud.

Kevin made a daylight trip to the cemetery to see the grave where Marsha Collins was buried. The grave rested in a new section of the cemetery, amid rolling hills with a pond. The grave had been freshly dug—dirt covered it, with no grass.

It would be easy to dig up, Kevin thought.

At a little past two in the morning, a car with its lights turned off drove through a back entrance to Cloverleaf Cemetery. It moved slowly down the one lane asphalt path toward the new section of the cemetery, pulling up thirty feet from the newly dug grave. The full moon that night provided enough light to find the grave without a flashlight. It was quiet—no one appeared to be in the cemetery. The cool night air had deposited a light frost on the grass. Kevin parked the car, opened the trunk, and pulled out a shovel and a tarp with a rope attached to one end. He closed the trunk and walked thirty feet to the freshly dug grave.

The dirt was loose and moist from a recent rain. Kevin looked in all directions to see if anyone was coming. Satisfied he was alone, he began digging. The damp dirt was heavy, making the digging slow and difficult. It took him over an hour to reach the surface of the casket, nearly six feet underground. It took another hour to expose the casket enough to be able to open the lid. Inside was the body of Marsha Colins, decayed and in a state of decomposition.

Damn, what a poor embalming job, Kevin thought.

He lifted the upper part of the body and carefully placed the tarp underneath. Then he lifted the lower body and pulled the remainder of the tarp down so it completely covered the back side of the corpse. The sides of the tarp were long enough to be able to wrap around the front of the corpse, allowing Kevin to completely wrap the body in the tarp. Then he tied a rope around the tarp and lifted the body from the casket. When he got the corpse completely out, Kevin closed the casket and began shoveling the dirt back into the grave.

The sun was beginning to come over the horizon by the time he had filled the hole. Kevin used the rope to pull the tarp back to his car. It was a slow process, and the sunlight made his deeds visible to anyone that came into the cemetery. Thirty minutes later, he lifted the tarp into the trunk of his car and closed it. He got into the car, took a deep breath of relief, started the engine, and drove off.

He had gotten to the exit when he saw the pick-up

truck in his rearview mirror. *It must be a cemetery worker's truck,* he thought.

Kevin had no idea if the driver of the truck saw him, but he wasn't going to concern himself with it. After all, he had a corpse in his trunk. All he could concern himself with now was getting away without getting caught. He needed to get the body home as soon as possible.

Then a sick feeling came over him. He had made a horrible mistake, a dumb mistake. He had left the shovel back at the grave site.

The sun was completely up by the time he got to his house. Kevin pulled the car into the garage, lifted the canvass with the body inside out of his trunk, and dragged it to a freezer on the other side of the garage. He lifted the lid, remove several packages of frozen meat and vegetables, and lifted the body up and dropped it inside. Then he placed the frozen food on top of the canvas and closed the lid. The freezer would keep the body fresh until he was ready to move it.

He would move the body to the basement of his mother's house later that evening. But for now, he would make breakfast, take a shower, and sleep. Grave digging was tiring work. He was dirty, tired, and hungry.

Kevin was sound asleep when the phone rang late that afternoon. It was Mike Malott. There was a head-on collision on Highway 71 just south of town, with multiple fatalities. Four of the bodies had been delivered to the funeral home. Kevin needed to go to work right away. It would be two more days before he was able to move the body to the basement at his mother's house.

He hadn't been to that house in months. Kevin hadn't talked to his brother since the day he left. He wasn't even sure the back door would be unlocked. He thought it would be—he had instructed Dennis to always leave it unlocked so he could enter and go to the basement whenever he wanted. Kevin didn't think Dennis would go against his wishes, but then again, Dennis had made it clear he didn't want to see Kevin again. He wanted him out of his life. If he meant it, he may have locked the door to prevent Kevin from entering the house.

Kevin pulled up the driveway and lifted Marsha's body out of the trunk, then dragged it to the back of the house. When he got to the back door, he took a deep breath and turned the door knob. The door opened—Dennis had left it unlocked. A smile came over Kevin's face. He dragged the body inside, opened the door leading to the basement, and pulled the body down the stairs, closing the door behind him.

The finished projects had been well-cared for. They had been dusted. They were organized. Even one-legged Earl had been cared for. Dennis had placed him in a special place in the basement, surrounded by other special projects.

Things in the basement were just like he had left them. Dennis had cared for them just like Kevin knew he would.

The newspapers called Kevin the Southside Vigilante. Clancy Arnold was his first victim. That's what they thought anyway. There would be many more. Kevin had never admitted to himself that he enjoyed killing. He had always told Dennis it was a means to an end.

"I'm a taxidermist and embalmer. Death is the only way I can apply my craft," he told Dennis.

But as a vigilante, murder became his craft. He enjoyed it. He craved it. He was proud of it. The news media fed his addiction to it. They encouraged it. The news media glorified his crimes.

***

Clancy Arnold's murder got the attention of Detective Will Baczenas. He became lead detective for that crime. Nobody knew it at that time, but that crime began the hunt for Kevin Collins.

He interviewed the woman in the truck with Clancy Arnold at the time of the killing. She did not see anything. It was too dark. She was pinned beneath her rapist.

He interviewed customers in the bar. They were not helpful.

He interviewed a maintenance worker that saw a car leaving the cemetery in the early morning hours of the crime. But he couldn't remember the make or color of the car.

"It was a small sedan," he said. That was all he remembered.

The case went nowhere. All the detective could do was wait for the next murder.

***

That would come soon enough. But first, Kevin had one more trophy for his basement. This would become his most cherished trophy.

After Marsha, he would bring his victims home with him. There would be no need to dig their bodies up.

Dennis was waiting for him in the basement.

"I've got a new project," Kevin said. "Are we good, little brother?"

"Yeah, just make sure Mother doesn't know you are down here. She's not doing well at all. Ever since Earl disappeared, she won't eat and she won't get out of bed. She's stopped talking to me. I'm scared she has given up."

"I'm sorry, Dennis. But you know we had no choice. We had to kill Earl."

"I know, Kevin. Just don't ever make me cut off a leg again. I'm still having nightmares about it."

"Damn, you're such a panzy, Dennis. It's a good thing you've got me around to do the things you don't have the stomach for. Can you unlock the room for me so I can carry her to my work bench?"

"Yeah, but who is the project?"

"You'll see. Just wait until I get her in the room and unwrap her from the tarp."

A few minutes later, Kevin placed the body on his work bench and slowly removed the tarp.

"Shit, Kevin. Is that who I think it is?" Dennis said when the body was unwrapped.

"It's my wife, Marsha," Kevin said with a smile on his face.

"What are you going to do with her? She's a mess."

"She's going to be my greatest project. She's going to be the queen of the basement."

"Why, Kevin?"

"Because I love her. I always have. Now she'll be with me. She wanted to leave me. Did I ever tell you that, Dennis?"

"No, you didn't."

"She was going to file for divorce. She was done with me. I couldn't let that happen. I loved her. She always had boyfriends. I knew that and accepted it. They were all losers. She always attracted the worst men, just like Mother. I used that to get to her. I befriended an ex-con I met at Kelly's. He needed money…he didn't have morals…he had killed before. I paid him to seduce her, to gain her confidence, to get into her bed. That was easier than I even imagined. He was exactly her type, young, handsome, and a loser. We set a plan for that night. It went exactly the way I wanted it to. He killed her just as I wanted. Then he went after her daughters. He had no idea I was waiting for him. He had no idea I wasn't going to let him leave that house alive. The plan was perfect. The police and that Detective Baczenas didn't even suspect me."

"But look at her, Kevin. She's been in that casket for months, and the damage to her head is tremendous. How are you going to make her presentable?"

"That's why she'll be my greatest project."

Kevin left her on the work bench. The sun was coming up. Mother would wake up soon. He didn't want her to know he was there. He would lock Marsha in the room and come back that night to begin his work on her.

CHAPTER 11
THE HUNT FOR A SERIAL KILLER

Kevin worked for four weeks on Marsha. He used every bit of his artistic skills to make her look as he remembered her. When finished, he created the perfect display for her in a special room he had built for his best completed projects.

When he was finished, it was time for him to find new projects.

Kevin went back to the bars, not Kelly's this time — he didn't want to chance being recognized. Kansas City was full of bars like Kelly's, neighborhood establishments in predominantly lower to middle income sections of town. People didn't ask questions in those type of bars. Kevin blended in. He could be a chameleon. People kept to themselves. They wouldn't think twice about a loner sitting by himself. Kevin could watch and wait until he found just the right person deserving of the basement.

He never spent more than a few nights in the same bar — he didn't want anyone to remember him. Sitting in a corner, back to a wall, he drank and watched. He was looking for a specific scenario that would allow him to act — an argument that erupted into a fight, a knife or a gun being pulled, someone being threatened. He wanted that same rush of adrenaline he'd felt when he dropped that tire iron on the rapist in Kelly's parking lot.

Kevin was addicted to murder. He had accepted that. But he wanted acceptance from others. Kevin wanted others to admire his skills. But he had always been afraid to let others know about his talents. That's why he darkened the windows in the basement. That's why he kept the door locked for his most prized finished projects. Dennis knew, but he was the only one. Kevin wanted desperately for others to admire his work. He feared he was an artist that would only be recognized for his talent after his death. That's why picking the right project now was so important. He needed to find someone that deserved to die, someone that others would be glad was gone, someone the news media would credit to the vigilante. Through them, his actions would be glorified. He would receive the acceptance he needed so badly, although he knew he could only be recognized for part of his talent. His greatest talent was in the way he brought his projects back to life in that basement. That talent had to go undiscovered for now. The public was not ready for it. They would not understand it. His finished projects, his great talent, would remain in the basement, hidden and unknown from others.

Kevin was seated in a corner of a small country bar on the north side of town. It was late, past one. He had been there for five hours. He was feeling no pain. Kevin could consume a lot of booze in five hours, and certainly had that night.

Jethro's Place was a small bar that had seen better days. Its clientele consisted mainly of bikers and blue-collar factory workers. The bar's business was dependent on several factories located just north of downtown. Their business increased dramatically as the shifts changed at the various factories in the area. There were about three dozen people in the bar at just past one, all white, all redneck.

The place went nearly silent. Everyone turned to look at the three young men that walked into the bar. They looked preppy with their designer jeans and tailored sports shirts.

They are either lost or too drunk to know they have stumbled in to a biker bar, Kevin thought.

By the way they staggered to the bar, Kevin knew it was the latter.

They are wasted, Kevin thought. *None of them look older than twenty-one.*

Kevin figured them for college students out on a bar cruise.

"Give us three Guinness drafts and three shots of Jack black," one of them said to the bartender.

The bartender, a middle-aged man with slightly graying hair greased back, with a pony tail flowing nine inches down his back, gave them a disgusted look. "We don't have any damn Guinness or any fucking Jack black. I can pour you a Pabst and give you shots of Old Crow, or you can turn around and get the hell out of here."

"Sorryyy," one of them said, stretching out the word to show his disdain for the bartender.

"Let's see some ID first," the bartender said.

The boys pulled out their driver's licenses and put

them on the bar.

The bartender looked at them, and without saying a word began pouring three glasses of Pabst.

One of the boys handed him a credit card to run a tab.

"We don't take credit cards here," the bartender said. "You'll need to pay in cash."

One of the boys pulled out a wad of twenties from his front right pocket and threw two of them on the bar. "That should take care of the first round," he said.

Kevin watched as several of the rednecks in the bar looked over the boys. Two of them moved on each side of them. Two others left the bar and went outside to the parking lot.

"Give us another round, bartender," one of the boys said.

One of the regulars that had taken a seat next to the boys leaned over the bar and said, "Give me a bottle of Old Crow, four glasses, and put the cost on the college boy's tab, Duane."

"What the fuck, man?" one of the boys said.

Kevin watched as one of the rednecks stood up and pulled out a knife from his front pocket.

"Hey man, we don't want any trouble."

"Then get the hell out of here."

The boys got up and walked out of the bar. The two rednecks followed them out.

Kevin took one last sip from his beer and walked out of the bar. When he got outside, he could see the boys cornered at the far end of the parking lot, surrounded by four rednecks — the two that confronted them in the bar and their two friends that had left the bar earlier. The boys were being robbed.

Kevin walked slowly to his car. He opened the trunk and pulled out a ski mask and put it on. Then he pulled out a gun, attached a silencer to the gun, and looked around the parking lot for any witnesses. He got in his car, started the engine, and drove slowly toward the group. He rolled down the window as he approached.

After robbing the three boys, their attackers stabbed one of them and began beating up the other two.

"Hey, asshole, turn those fucking headlights off," one of them said as the car approached.

Kevin rolled down the window and stopped his car just a few feet away from the group. Their victims were laying on the ground, their attackers standing over them, when Kevin pointed the gun out the open window.

"Leave them alone," he yelled.

"Who the fuck are you?" one of them shouted back.

Kevin moved the barrel of the gun toward him and fired three quick shots.

He fell to the ground. The other three attackers took off running.

Engine still running, Kevin got out of the car to check on the three boys. One was bleeding a lot from a knife wound. The other two had been beaten but were not seriously hurt.

Then Kevin checked on the redneck he had shot. Three quick shots, all landing within inches of each other near the heart. He was dead. Kevin dragged him to his trunk and lifted him inside and drove away. A few blocks away, he stopped to call 911 to report the three injured boys. The conversation was very short, not long enough to trace. He gave no details, just to say an ambulance was needed at Jethro's Place on Route 29.

Kevin drove to his mother's house. He backed the car in next to the garage and carried the body to the back of the house.

"I've got another project," he told Dennis. "Take care of this one until I have time to work on him."

The news media spent several days talking about the vigilante that had come to the rescue of the three college students. They interviewed the three boys, customers in the bar that night, and Detective Baczenas. They glorified the acts of the vigilante. They made him sound like a hero.

Kevin loved every minute of it. He felt like his life had a more meaningful purpose. He felt good about what he had done. Dennis was proud of his brother.

***

Will Baczenas was determined to find the vigilante. This time he had made mistakes. He had left evidence. One of the bullets had gone through the victim and was found in the parking lot. They matched it to a 9mm handgun with a .45 suppressor. Gun records were checked and cross checked against purchasers of that type of weapon.

In addition, customers in the bar had noticed the young man seated in a corner of the bar that had left right after the boys and their attackers. A sketch artist made a composite photo based on witnesses and the drink server's description of the man.

Witnesses described the car the vigilante drove. The evidence was not enough to find the vigilante, but it narrowed the field.

Detective Baczenas now had two killings on his

plate tied to the vigilante. The news media had brought a lot of attention to his crimes. There was pressure to find the vigilante before he could act again. Detective Baczenas was provided a task force of three — one other detective named Detective Moffit, and two seasoned street cops — to help track the vigilante. He had few clues and no suspects. The only common denominator in the two murders was that they occurred at bars.

The vigilante must have witnessed a confrontation in the bar and followed the attackers when they left, the detective thought. *Bars have been his hunting ground so far. He must not be a regular customer because none of the witnesses recognized him. The other unusual thing about these crimes is that the murders occurred at bars in two different parts of the city, nearly thirty miles away from each other. The bars were much different too, one a solid stripper's bar known for prostitution just off the interstate in the far southwest corner of the city, the other a biker bar in a crime-ridden section of the city.*

Detective Baczenas was a seasoned veteran of the police department. His experience was that criminals tended to perform their crimes in areas they were familiar with. *The two parts of the city where these vigilante acts took place were so socially and economically unique to each other that it was highly doubtful the perpetrator was familiar with both,* he thought.

"That was unusual but not totally unique, particularly for a vigilante," he told members of his task force. "A vigilante goes to areas where he has the best opportunity to act on a crime. The biker bar was in that type of area. Where we need to concentrate our efforts is with the first murder. That was likely done as an impulse act, in a bar and area where the vigilante either lives or frequents."

Detective Baczenas was very familiar with Kelly's — he had been there nearly a dozen times over the years. He had two unsolved crimes that occurred there. The first was the disappearance of Barbara Johnson, a dancer at the club and a suspected prostitute. The crime had occurred nearly two years earlier. It was a cold case now. Clues to her disappearance had gone nowhere.

"She's just another hooker that ran away," his supervisor had told him when he requested the detective to close the case.

Detective Baczenas felt otherwise. Coworkers, friends and family that the detective interviewed never heard from her. She never returned to her apartment, and her clothes and other possessions were never taken. She left her purse and several hundred dollars in her apartment. She simply disappeared. There was evidence she went to a hotel room with a man. Detectives Baczenas and Moffit interviewed him but found no evidence he had done anything to her. He remembered how peculiar the man seemed. His gut told him there was something odd about his behavior. He seemed nervous. The detective had the feeling he was hiding something. But without a body and without any proof of a crime, the disappearance of Barbara Johnson became a cold case.

Still, this latest crime might warrant opening that cold case file. Another interview with the man that was last seen with Barbara Johnson needed to be done.

There is probably no connection, the detective thought. *But it's better to be thorough.*

He assigned reopening the Barbara Johnson file to Detective Moffit.

Two days later, Detective Moffit stopped him. "We need to talk about the Barbara Johnson case," he said. "I think I've found something important."

"Okay, what is it?"

"The man that rented the hotel room and was the last to see Barbara Johnson was Dennis Collins. Does that name ring a bell?"

"Yes, it does. I remember interviewing him. So what?"

"I crossed referenced the name and the address in our database to see if there had been any other police calls, complaints, or investigations involving that name or address."

"Okay, so what did you find?"

"His father died in the house from a fall down the basement stairs six years ago. Also, Dennis Collins was interviewed about the disappearance of a local elderly woman and several pets in the neighborhood about four years ago."

"Okay, I'll admit that is odd, but I don't see where it ties into the disappearances at Kelly's."

Detective Moffit smiled and said, "I'll admit there is no direct connection, but I found something else interesting.

"What?"

"When I ran the last name 'Collins,' I got a hit on a Kevin Collins, also."

"Who the hell is Kevin Collins?"

"He evidently is the brother of Dennis Collins. Do you remember any mention of a brother when you interviewed Dennis Collins?"

"No, I don't."

"There are no notes in the file that mention a Kevin Collins," Detective Moffit said.

"So, what did you find on Kevin Collins?"

"Do you remember the grave robbery a few months back where the shovel was left at the grave?"

"Yes, I remember. Marsha Collins, I believe, was the grave that was robbed."

"Yes, Marsha was Kevin Collin's wife. Don't you find the connection to be a little suspicious?"

"I think we need to look a little deeper into Dennis Collins," Detective Baczenas said.

"Do we have a photo of Dennis Collins in the file?"

"Yes, we do."

"Why don't you take it down to Kelly's and see if anyone recognizes him?"

"I'll talk to his brother, Kevin, again. Maybe he can shed some light on his brother. There was something odd about Dennis that I remember from the interview at his mother's house. He seemed nervous, like he wasn't being totally honest," Detective Baczenas said. "Let's see if we can dig enough information on him to get a warrant to search the house."

The doorbell rang at Kevin's house at ten minutes past three the next afternoon. He was sound asleep. It took three separate rings and several loud knocks on the door for him to wake up. He was wearing his pajamas when he opened the door a few minutes later.

"Mr. Collins, may we come in?" Detective Baczenas asked.

"Sure, I guess. What do you want?"

"We just need to ask you a few more questions about the disappearance of your wife's body."

"Okay, Detectives. But I'm not sure that I can be of any more help than the last time we spoke."

"Maybe not, but we would appreciate a few more minutes of your time. Can we come in and sit?"

"Yes, certainly."

The two detectives walked into the living room and took seats in chairs on the opposite side of each other. Kevin took a seat on the couch between the two men.

"Mr. Collins, do you have a brother named Dennis?"

"Yes, Detective. He is my younger brother. Is he in some sort of trouble?"

"No," Detective Baczenas said. "Like I said, we are following up on the disappearance of your wife's body from the cemetery. Would your brother have any reason to remove your wife's body?"

"No. That's crazy. He would never do anything like that. Where did you get an idea like that?"

"We're just following up all possible leads. Mr. Collins, were you aware that your brother had frequented a strip club named Kelly's, and that he went back to a hotel room with one of the dancers who disappeared later that night?"

"No, I wasn't aware of that. Dennis and I have a bit of a strained relationship. We don't talk to each other much anymore."

"When was the last time you saw your brother?"

"Probably a month or so ago."

"What did you talk about?"

"Nothing really. I went to the house to pick up some

tools I'd left there. He met me at the door. We really didn't talk about anything. I told him what I needed, he got them for me, and I left. What's this all about, Detectives? Do you suspect my brother in the woman's disappearance? Because I can't imagine him hurting anybody."

"No, we're just investigating right now. A car similar to the type your brother owns was seen leaving the cemetery where your wife's body was removed, and a credit card receipt and eyewitness statements place your brother in the hotel room with a dancer at Kelly's the night she disappeared. We find those two circumstances worth investigating."

"Well, I can assure you, Detectives, that my brother had nothing to do with either situation. He would never disturb my wife's burial plot. Why would he? That's crazy. And as for the woman that disappeared, you've got to understand that Dennis wouldn't hurt a fly. He's timid and socially awkward, but he would never hurt anyone."

"Mr. Collins," Detective Baczenas said. "What did you and your brother fight about that caused you to stay away from him so long?"

"We argued over our mother. Dennis rarely leaves the house because he is constantly taking care of her. I was trying to help him. He needs to get away from her sometimes. He needs his own life. She is draining the life out of him."

"Why don't you talk to your mother about that?"

"I'm afraid I haven't spoken to Mother in years, Detectives. We had a falling out right after Father died. In a way, she blamed me for his death. I moved out of the house soon after his death, and we haven't spoken since."

"Why did your mother blame you, Mr. Collins?"

"I've always been the black sheep of the family—a disappointment to them, I guess. Our father was a drunk and a violent person, Detectives. He preyed on the weak. Mother was weak, and so was Dennis. He physically and emotionally abused them on a regular basis. But I wasn't weak. I stood up to him. I tried to protect Mother and Dennis. The night Father died he had been abusive. I stood up to him. He got terribly angry and came after me. I was afraid he'd kill me. I ran into the kitchen and hid. He chased after me. When he couldn't find me, I guess he thought I had run down to the basement. He opened the door and started to run down. That's when he fell. Mother never forgave me. As much as my father beat her and abused her, she still loved him. I've never been able to figure that out."

"One last question, Mr. Collins. Has your brother ever mentioned going to a bar call Jethro's Place?"

"No, Detective."

"Thanks, Mr. Collins," Detective Baczenas said as he and Detective Moffit stood up. "I think that is all the questions we have for right now."

The detectives walked out the door and got into their unmarked police car.

"Did you write everything down, Mike?"

"Yes, I took notes on everything he said," Detective Moffit replied.

"There's something odd about him, and certainly about his brother." Detective Baczenas said. "Did you notice how unemotional he seemed, particularly about the grave robbery of his wife?"

"He didn't seem to care."

The detectives left the house and went back to the police station. Detective Baczenas wanted to meet with his team, compare notes, and determine the next steps.

Officers Conner and Mathews were given the task of interviewing customers and staff at both Kelly's and Jethro's Place. They had taken the picture of Dennis Collins from the old case file and showed it to everyone they interviewed. Detective Baczenas was anxious to hear what they'd discovered.

"All right, Officers, tell me what you found out."

Brian Connor, the senior of the two officers, spoke up. "The picture is old and faded, so it made identification difficult. But the server at Kelly's thought she recognized the picture as a customer that ran up a bar tab the night Barbara Johnson disappeared."

"That's not news, Officer," Detective Baczenas said. "We have already determined that Dennis Collins was in the bar that night, and that he took Barbara Johnson to a hotel room."

"Yes, I know," Officer Conner said. "But the server remembered more than serving Dennis Collins drinks. She remembered some rather odd behavior from him."

"What?"

"He seemed to be carrying on a conversation with someone at the table. But no one was there other than him."

"Was he talking to himself?"

"No, the server didn't think so. He was looking toward an empty chair. He seemed agitated. The server said she felt something was wrong with him. She wasn't afraid of him— she didn't think he was violent, but she thought he was a little crazy. Whenever she got close, the conversation would stop. But when she was farther away, she could see him gesturing and talking to the empty chair across from him."

"What did he say?" Detective Baczenas asked.

"She couldn't make most of it out, certainly not enough to determine what the conversation was about. But she did hear a name. He called the person he appeared to be talking to Kevin. She heard him use that name several times."

CHAPTER 12
PROJECTS IN THE BASEMENT

The basement had become a crowded place. Dennis spent much of his days caring for the completed projects and organizing the basement. One hidden room just off the room with the cages was occupied with the special projects, the trophies of Kevin's work, the best of the best. The room was built with no windows, its walls painted black. The floors were covered with thick, red carpeting. The room was well insulated to keep it seven degrees warmer than the rest of the basement, a temperature Kevin requested to preserve the completed projects in their ideal state.

The centerpiece, the crowning jewel of the room, was Marsha. Her state of decompensation when she was unearthed from her grave required every bit of Kevin's talent and embalming knowledge to preserve. She was his greatest accomplishment. Standing a few feet away from her was Belinda, who looked amazing, like Marsha. She had been the jewel of the room until Marsha was completed. Earl Chase, mother's fiancé, was there. His death had driven a wedge between Dennis and Kevin for some time. It had traumatized their mother and sent her into a spiraling depression. He was the only one-legged trophy in the basement, a masterpiece of work for Kevin. Also in the room was Mary Brown, Kevin's first human project. She was also the least artistic of Kevin's works, but she held a special place in his heart since she was his first. He often came in the room to look at her, to learn from her flaws, to make his future works better. Barbara Johnson was another prized piece of work. Dennis had left her in the trunk of his car for four days.

"Thank God Detective Bacenas never searched your car," Kevin had said to him.

She was in poor condition when Kevin found her. He made her look alive again, even better than he remembered her from her last night at Kelly's. Dennis had become rather violent with her. Her clothes were ruined, torn and blood-stained. Kevin had gone out shopping to Victoria's Secret for clothes similar to the ones she was wearing that night. All the trophies in that room were dressed just like the brothers remembered them. Clothes that were soiled or torn or bloodied were replaced with new clothes. Their hair was done, make-up was applied. Kevin spared no detail to present his trophies as they appeared the last night they were alive.

Kevin installed special lighting in the room that enhanced viewing. One switch controlled dozens of lights positioned strategically in the room. When Kevin or Dennis were not in the room, the lights were off, the room was completely dark, and the door leading into the room was locked.

The rest of the basement housed the less special trophies. Each species was organized in their own section. They were kept separate from their natural predators. Kevin had told Dennis many years earlier, "I want their afterlife to be peaceful and non-threatening. I want them away from the predators they feared during their life."

Kevin believed the time they spent in the basement was only temporary. Their physical presence would always remain in the basement, but their souls would venture on to another life. He wanted to make them as comfortable as possible until their souls departed their bodies.

The basement contained every project Kevin had ever completed, from the very first small creatures to the cats and the dogs to the humans. Every phase of his progress over the years was documented in that basement. It was a showcase for him. But there was one thing about the basement that bothered Kevin, one thing he thought about almost every day. His life work was in that basement. Every bit of his artistic talent was reflected in the finished projects he housed downstairs. Yet only he and Dennis had ever seen them. They were the only two people alive in the world that knew how great his skills were. They were works of art, fitting of any museum. Kevin's talents were not being recognized by the outside world. To others, he was no more than an embalmer, a funeral director, an everyday person. He wanted so badly to be recognized for his work. But to be recognized also meant to be misunderstood, to be judged for the means to the end, not the end product.

"Sure, people had to give up their lives to be memorialized eternally in that basement. But their lives were pretty meaningless anyway," he would tell his brother. "I never killed anyone that didn't deserve it. They all had better lives waiting for them in their afterlife."

The end result justified the means used to get there, he thought.

Kevin rationalized everything he did. He enjoyed killing, but it wasn't an addiction that he couldn't stop if he wanted to. His art, the work he did in the basement, was the addiction he couldn't give up. As soon as one trophy was completed, he had to start work on another. He had over two-hundred trophies in that basement. They spanned every wall, most on shelves three to five levels tall going from floor to ceiling.

With his last trophy, the biker from Jethro's Place, completed, it was time to start searching for the next project. Kevin would need to be more careful now. The police had paid him a visit. They weren't suspicious of him, but they were suspicious of Dennis.

Dennis has never been very bright, he thought. *He is soft. He makes mistakes. He would fold under questioning.*

Kevin wasn't worried about himself. He didn't make mistakes. He was smarter than the detectives that came to his door. Kevin would never get caught. But Dennis was different. He would crack under pressure. Dennis was the weak link in the two brothers, and would turn on Kevin to save himself. He had to keep Dennis away from the police for now, until he had a plan, until he could safely eliminate the only witness to his crime.

Kevin didn't tell his brother about the visit from the two detectives.

It would only make him worry, make him more nervous than he already is. He might even decide to turn on me,, to tell the police what I've done, Kevin thought.

Kevin would move back into the house, into the basement. He would tell Dennis not to answer the door, not to pick up the phone. Dennis always did what Kevin told him. He would keep Dennis in that house, out of sight, away from others.

It is for his own good, Kevin justified. *If the police come to the door or call, they can talk to me.*

He would only need to hide his brother for a short time, until he had a plan for a permanent solution. Dennis had served his purpose. He was a good soldier, never arguing, never resisting what Kevin told him. But if someone needed to be sacrificed to keep Kevin safe, Dennis would need to be that sacrificial lamb.

Kevin moved into the basement. He spent his days there, watching his brother, controlling him. Days went by with no visits or phone calls from the police.

Maybe their leads dried up. Maybe they aren't going to talk to Dennis, Kevin thought. But he quickly dismissed those thoughts. He had sized Detective Baczenas up the second he met him. He wasn't the type of person to give up—he would work every lead until he had the answers. He hadn't contacted Dennis because he didn't have all the answers. When he did, he would come for his brother. Kevin couldn't let that occur.

Soon after moving back into the basement, Kevin started searching for his next project.

A wise man would stop killing, Kevin told himself. But he couldn't stop. It was necessary to feed his need to create his masterpieces in the basement, an addiction as strong as any opioid. He was more careful now. Mistakes had been made before that led the police to his door. He couldn't let that happen again.

He would not go into bars this time in search of his next project.

There are too many potential witnesses in bars, and more people mean a greater chance of being identified, Kevin thought.

Besides, Kevin had a drinking problem. He knew it. Drinking softened his intelligence. It made him more likely to make a mistake. He could give up drinking — he couldn't give up killing. Watching the last few seconds of life drain from a victim's eyes was just too strong of a pull for him.

The north downtown streets of Kansas City where the hookers walked and the homeless lived would be his prowling ground. He drove Dennis's car to do his hunting.

The police already suspected Dennis. If someone got suspicious and wrote down the license plate number everything would track back to him, Kevin reasoned.

Kevin looked for the most vulnerable victims — the ones that wouldn't be missed, the ones that were alone, the ones that would come to him, a complete stranger, for help or a few dollars. He didn't even need to get out of his car. He would entice them with money or food or clothing. They would enter his car counting on a stranger's generosity.

They would never leave that car. Kevin's stun gun and sleeping pills assured that. He would drive them back to the house, drag them into the basement, take them to the locked room, and put them in a cage. Night after night he did that, until all eight cages in the basement were full.

Kevin chose to keep them alive until the excitement of watching their fear dissipated. He spent hours each day watching them, enjoying their suffering and fantasizing about their death. Kevin quit his job. His entire life now revolved around his projects. He would spend his future days in that basement with his projects. He slept and ate there. The only time he left the basement was to hunt for new projects. His demons had taken control of his life, the darkness inside of him now dominating his life.

***

Dennis did everything his brother told him. He took care of the projects, both the living ones and the dead. He fed them, cleaned them, and cared for them. Dennis was their only hope of surviving. When he wasn't caring for them, he took care of Mother. She was completely bedridden now. He fed and clothed her, he cleaned her and bathed her. He sat and talked to her. She rarely talked back. Her mind and body were nearly gone. Every minute of his day was spent caring for the projects and his mother. The only time he left the house was to get groceries or medication or supplies his brother requested.

Dennis felt empathy for the living projects that lived in the cages in the basement. He consoled them, assuring them that everything would be all right even though he knew it wouldn't. Dennis gave them hope. He was only trying to keep them as comfortable as possible until Kevin was ready for them. Because even though he felt empathy for the victims, he would never go against Kevin's wishes. Dennis had always been and would always be a loyal brother.

Eight women occupied the cages in the basement, each

handcuffed with their legs tied. Each cage was six feet long, four feet wide, and four feet high, just enough room to sit up or lay down, but not enough room to move about. The cages were lined against two opposite sides of the room, providing each victim a view of most of the other victims. Most hours they were heavily sedated, and slept from afternoon to the next morning. But Kevin insisted that they be awake every morning. That was when he watched them. By eight every day he pulled up a chair in the center of the room, drank a cup of black coffee, read the newspaper, and waited for his victims to wake up. One by one they would. Dennis stopped giving them sedation at eight every night, assuring that they would wake sometime the next morning.

That was Kevin's time with them. He never spoke to them. He never reacted to them. He just watched and listened. His adrenalin pumped as he watched the fear in their eyes, as he listened to the pain in their voices. Some cursed him. Some begged him to let them go. Most cried. All screamed. The room was soundproof. No one could hear them nor their screams, so their resistance only excited Kevin more.

He never showed emotion. He never talked to them. He never reacted to anything they said. He just sat and watched.

At noon precisely, every day, his emotional torture of them ended. He stood up and walked out the door without saying a word. Thirty minutes later, Dennis would enter with food and water. He unlocked the cages, one at a time, and fed the victims. It was their only meal of the day. When they were done eating, he cleaned them, removed the bucket each was given to relieve themselves, and replaced it with a clean bucket. After caring for them, he sedated each one, then sat in the same chair his brother had sat in and waited for each to fall asleep.

There was something about Dennis that made each of the victims feel that he was incapable of hurting them. There was something about him that gave them hope, something about him that made them feel he would protect them, that there was more good in him than bad. They opened up to him about themselves, about their families, about their desire to stay alive. As fearful as they were of Kevin, they were equally trusting in Dennis.

None of the victims had any idea why they were being held or what their ultimate fate would be. They voiced that to Dennis every day. He assured them that no harm would come to them. They wanted to believe him.

None of the victims were physically abused. Kevin had plans for them. He didn't want any of his projects damaged. But the psychological abuse each of them endured was horrendous.

***

After holding the victims for a week, the excitement had evaporated for Kevin. He had fed off his victims' fear, but that had leveled off. Many were starting to lose hope. The fear in their eyes had softened. It was replaced by a vacant stare, a hopelessness that showed no emotion.

Kevin wanted to bring that fear back. So, one morning after his victims had awakened, he got up from his chair, walked to the hidden door at the back of the room, and unlocked and opened it. The people in the cages followed him with their eyes. He turned to them and smiled. It was the first sign of emotion they had seen from him since their captivity.

It was an unsettling smile.

He walked over to one cage. A young girl, maybe eighteen-years-old, with freckles and short red hair, was inside. She had been a prostitute. He figured her for a runaway.

She was not meant for a life on the streets, he thought when he first saw her.

The girl was desperate. She needed to eat. She'd needed shelter when he spotted her. Money from selling her body would provide that. The young runaway didn't think she had any other choice. Kevin was one of her first customers. He looked married and in need of a little companionship. She sized him up quickly when he pulled up next to her. He looked harmless. She was wrong. The girl realized that a few minutes after getting into his car. He locked the door and pulled out the stun gun. She didn't even have time to scream.

She missed her family and wished she had never run away from home. She had told Dennis that many times. Her name was Rachel. Rachel was different from the others in the basement. She was so young, so innocent — she had her whole life in front of her. Rachel didn't come from an abusive home. Her parents were loving and God-fearing Christians, she told Dennis. Rachel was sure she had broken their hearts when she ran off.

Rachel was madly in love with a married man twelve-years older than her. He promised to leave his wife. They ran off together, but less than a week later he left her and went back to his wife. She was left on her own with no money in a strange city, trying desperately to hold on to her pride. She just couldn't go back to her parents, not after what she had done.

Rachel was breaking down faster than the others in the basement. She cried all day. Her body shook with fear. She was chosen by Kevin that morning because he needed someone to break, and she was the most fragile.

He stood over her, smiling.

"No, stay away from me," she screamed.

He began pulling her cage toward the secret room. She screamed. She resisted, but her hands and feet were bound. There was nothing she could do.

The others watched as he pulled her cage closer and closer to the room.

He pulled the cage inside the room, where it was pitch black. The cage disappeared into the darkness of the room. They could no longer see her, but they could hear her screams. The door shut behind them. For just a few seconds there was complete silence. Then a light came on, shining a ray of intense white light through the small opening between the floor and bottom of the door.

A few seconds later, a blood-curdling scream came from the room, from the girl. The scream seemed to go on for minutes, loud and deep, followed by complete silence.

A few minutes later the light went off underneath the door. The door opened and Kevin pulled the cage back to its spot in the other room. Rachel was still inside the cage, but she may as well have died in that secret room. Her will to live was gone. Her mind was empty. She was a shell of the person she had been. She would not speak, would not eat. What she had seen in that secret room had caused her to give up any hope of leaving that basement, and had ended her will to live. The others had seen it in her face. They now realized the evil in that basement was greater than anything they had imagined.

Rachel's trip into the secret room had served its purpose. The others in the cages were more frightened than before. The fear in their eyes was more intense, their cries more desperate. They had no idea what was in that room, and they didn't want to know. Their fight was back for a while. What Kevin did was emotional torture. He did it to prolong their suffering and to feed his need to relish in their fear.

Dennis asked him once why he took Rachel into that room.

"That room showcases my greatest accomplishments, my best artistic work. I wanted someone to see my finished projects. Until now, only you and I have seen the inside of that room. I wanted someone to know that their afterlife will be greater than the life they have had. They have seen how well we take care of them and how beautiful I make them. They have suffered in life. They won't suffer in death."

***

Dennis understood his brother, but he didn't agree with him. They were two totally different personalities with two different moral compasses. He wished he could stop his brother. He wished he could help the people in the cages, but he was weak. Kevin controlled him, much like his father had controlled his mother. Dennis was afraid of him, but more so than that, he was desperate for his brother's acceptance.

In all the years his mother and father were married, he never once heard his father say he loved his wife. She said it to him all the time. She accepted his drinking and his temper just to feel needed. Dennis was the same way with his brother.

He needed to feel needed. He needed to feel loved. So even though he didn't agree with it, even though it went against his moral compass, Dennis did exactly what his brother told him to do.

The mood in the room with the cages changed after Rachel was taken into the secret room. The others fought at first, but with time, they began to lose hope. A darkness engulfed that room, a smell of impending death.

With hope gone, the people in the cages stopped resisting their fate. The fear in their eyes, their screams, their tears all stopped, and Kevin quickly lost interest in them. Every few days he instructed Dennis to poison one of the women. He let Dennis choose the victim. He would mix arsenic in the water and food of the victim he picked. Late that night, after the chosen one succumbed to the poison, Dennis would remove them from the cage and take them to Kevin's workbench. The remaining people were heavily sedated, and not aware of what had happened to the chosen one.

One by one, the people in the cages disappeared and took their place in the secret room.

As others were chosen, Rachel remained alive. Dennis would select her last. He had empathized with her more than the others. Dennis had a connection with her, some sort of emotional bond. He had always spent more time with her than the others. Dennis took better care of her, fed her more than the others. Rachel was special, different from the others. He had developed feelings for her. In a way, she reminded Dennis of himself. She was weaker than the others. She had a good heart but had done bad things. Rachel was more innocent than the others,

Dennis had never had a girlfriend. He had never been on a date, but there was something about Rachel that made everything seem good.

After her trip into the special room, Rachel's mind left her. She no longer talked. Her eyes stared into empty space, and she wouldn't eat or drink. Dennis spent hours each day talking to her, feeding her and caring for her. She eventually came out of her stupor, and they began talking to each other. Rachel talked about her family in Chicago and about the boyfriend that used her and then left. She had so many regrets. Rachel wanted desperately to see her family again.

Dennis listened to her. He was a good listener. His feelings for her strengthened each day. She appeared to like him, to need him to be dependent on him, much like his mother had for so many years.

But with the disappearance of each additional person from their cage, Rachel became more desperate. She begged Dennis to let her go. She begged him to protect her from Kevin. He promised her that she would be safe. But he had promised that to the others, also, and now many of them were gone.

"I won't let my brother hurt you, Rachel," he said.

"Please let me go, Dennis. I won't tell anyone," she said.

Dennis knew he couldn't let her go. He couldn't go against Kevin no matter what his heart told him.

CHAPTER 13
TWO INVESTIGATIONS

Detective Baczenas was known for solving crimes and closing cases. He was the most seasoned and successful detective on the Kansas City police force. He was like a dog with a bone, never letting go until there was nothing left to chew on.

But now, he found himself with two investigations with no bodies, and few witnesses.

The vigilante murders occupied most of his time now. His superiors had demanded that. The vigilante was making the police department look bad. He was in the papers and on the news every night, and had gained the support and admiration of the people in Kansas City.

He was embarrassing the police department. Detective Baczenas was given a task force to find the vigilante. Every attack on a suspected criminal was credited to the vigilante. People wanted to believe that someone was doing what the police were incapable of.

And although Detective Baczenas was only able to credit two murders to the vigilante, the news media gave the vigilante credit for seven.

There were no solid clues to who the vigilante was. There were witnesses to the murders, and vague descriptions of the vigilante. There was a description of the car he drove. But there were no fingerprints or DNA to tie anyone to the crimes. Hell, there wasn't even a body left at the scene of the crime. That was what puzzled the task force the most.

Why does the vigilante take the body away after killing them, and what does he do with the body? were questions asked over and over again by Detective Baczenas.

While the police department used every resource available to find the vigilante, the crimes that concerned Detective Baczenas the most were being ignored. For nearly ten years, people had been disappearing. Detective Baczenas had begun investigating the disappearances when he was assigned to the Barbara Johnson case. But it wasn't long before he discovered other disappearances going back nearly ten years. There were similarities in those cases that made him suspect he was looking for one serial killer responsible for at least a dozen disappearances over the years.

The detective had no clue who the vigilante was. But he suspected that Dennis Collins was responsible for some of the disappearances. Problem was that he didn't have enough evidence to arrest him. The investigation had centered on Dennis for the past several weeks. There was plenty of circumstantial evidence that he was involved in three disappearances, but no bodies were ever found. Detective Baczenas was also certain that Dennis was the person that dug up Marsha Collins's grave. He had a partial fingerprint match on a shovel left at the grave, but, why he did it and where the body was remained a mystery.

He remained puzzled about something else, too. In the disappearance of Barbara Johnson, the server at Kelley's said he appeared to be talking to someone else, although no one was seated next to him. She said he was talking to Kevin.

Kevin is his brother's name. Was he talking to his brother or someone else named Kevin? the detective wondered.

The detective had not interviewed Dennis Collins. He chose to wait until he had some shred of evidence that a crime had been committed. People disappeared all the time. That didn't mean they had met with foul play.

Barbara Johnson's disappearance is the key, he thought.

She had friends. She had a family. Barbara was missed. She disappeared without a trace. Her purse and belongings were left behind. Barbara had a bank account that was never touched after her disappearance.

Two days after her disappearance, Detective Baczenas had requested a search warrant for Dennis Collins's residence. The judge denied his request, citing no evidence that a crime had been committed.

"She's a prostitute," he was told. "Prostitutes disappear all the time. They get sick of the business and run away."

Detective Baczenas didn't believe that. But with no additional evidence of a crime, he was unable to get a search warrant. And without a search warrant, the case of Barbara Johnson's disappearance dried up.

There were times the bureaucracy of the police department made him sick. This was one of those times.

Publicity about the vigilante had made the case top priority. Every day the detective had to report on the case's progress. He was told to put other open cases on a back burner and to work exclusively on the vigilante case.

He was told to turn his other cases over to other detectives. He did as he was told, except for the Barbara Johnson investigation. He refused to turn that case over.

"That crime also happened in Kelly's. We haven't ruled out a connection between the vigilante murder and Barbara Johnson's disappearance," he told his supervisor. "I want to continue exploring leads from that case until we determine there is or is not a connection."

Detective Baczenas didn't believe in coincidences. The crimes happened within a year of each other at a bar that had not experienced any major crimes before. Detective Baczenas couldn't shake the feeling that the two incidents were somehow tied together. He had tried to find evidence that there was a connection between the two crimes, but he found nothing.

He was confident that if foul play happened to Barbara Johnson, Dennis Collins did it. But he was unable to place Dennis Collins in the bar the night of the vigilante murder. It was true that the description of the car the vigilante left in matched the car registered to Dennis Collins. But there were a lot of dark, older model Fords registered in Kansas City. Without a license plate number, it was impossible to trace that car back to Dennis Collins.

His task team had shown Dennis Collins's picture in that bar, and also Jethro's Place, where the other vigilante killing took place. But no one could say with certainty that he was the vigilante, or even that he was in either bar that night.

As he told his task force, "In both vigilante murders, witnesses were close enough to get a good look at the killer, but their descriptions of him were vague and varied between witnesses. Composite sketches made after the murders didn't match. They weren't even close."

For a while the police thought the vigilante murders were done by two different people. But shoe imprints and tire marks left in the parking lot of both bars appeared to match. There were two other crucial pieces of information that supported the theory that the same person committed both vigilante acts. Partial fingerprints left at both crime scenes matched. Detective Baczenas had the fingerprints run through the criminal database, but there were no matches. The other crucial piece of information that tied the two crimes together was a match book that was found in the parking lot of Jethro's Place near the murder scene—a match book with Kelly's logo on the cover. A partial fingerprint was taken from it also, and it matched the others found at the crime scene.

Detective Baczenas had solved nearly every case he was ever given. With his vast experience, he was confident that with diligence and determination these crimes would be solved also.

Still, a little luck would be nice, he thought.

That luck would come a few days later. When there were no matches of the fingerprints in the criminal database, Detective Baczenas ordered that the fingerprints be run through both the criminal database and the unsolved crimes database on a monthly basis, hoping that fingerprints from a recent crime or arrest might match with the vigilante's prints.

Detective Moffitt gave him the good news.

"We have a match," he said, running into Detective Baczena's office. "We have a match on the vigilante fingerprints with another crime."

"Tell me about it."

"Remember the grave robbery a few months ago?"

"Yes, what about it?"

"The shovel. The shovel that was left at the grave. It had fingerprints on it. They must have been slow getting them entered into the database, but they're in the system now. The fingerprints on that shovel matched the fingerprints left at the vigilante murder scenes."

"No shit. So, the person that dug up the body of Marsha Collins is our vigilante. I know who the vigilante is," Detective Baczenas said. "I don't have proof, but I know who he is."

Detective Bacenas set out to get the evidence he would need to arrest Dennis Collins. He ordered around the clock surveillance of the house where Dennis Collins lived.

"If he buys a cup of coffee, a soft drink, a sandwich, if he smokes a cigarette, anything he touches and throws away, I want you to grab it and bring it in. We'll run the fingerprints and see if we get a match," he told his team.

That same night, the surveillance began. For three days, no one left the house. At nearly one in the morning on the fourth day, the garage door opened and a dark blue Ford Tauris pulled out of the garage, turned around, and went down the driveway. Detective Moffit sat in an unmarked police car parked on the street fifty feet from the driveway. He couldn't tell who was driving the car, but as soon as it turned onto the street, he followed. He kept his headlights turned off as long as he could — the streets were nearly empty that time of the night. But when the Taurus took the ramp to Hwy 71, the detective was forced to turn his headlights on. The car traveled north on Hwy 71 to East Hwy 270. Detective Moffit stayed a safe distance behind so as not to be spotted.

He watched as the Taurus drove north on Hwy 270 and turned west on Highway 70 toward downtown. Just east of downtown, the car turned north again. Detective Moffit knew this area well. It was the old warehouse district, where the homeless lived and the prostitutes walked the streets. Three blocks from the highway, the detective lost sight of the Taurus. There were few cars on the streets. He watched for headlights and taillights, but the few cars he saw were not Fords.

He turned down north 5th Street and saw a car ahead, pulled over to the curb. He couldn't make out the type of car. The detective turned off his headlights and slowly moved down the street. When his car got within a hundred feet of the parked car, he could make out a woman — a hooker, it appeared, based on her leather mini-skirt and bright red halter-top — talking to someone through the passenger window.

There were no other cars on the road. The detective pulled within sixty-feet of the car and stopped. He didn't want to be spotted. There were no streetlights, no building lights. It was completely dark on the street, making it impossible to identify the person driving the car. He couldn't even be sure the car was the same one that left Dennis Collins's house nearly an hour earlier. It was a small car, dark colored and an older model. He was fairly certain it was a Ford Taurus, but he wasn't completely sure. He was too far away to read the license plate. He could tell there was one person in the car.

A few seconds later, the passenger car door opened and the woman got inside. There was a short conversation, and then the car began to drive off. The detective followed with his headlights turned off. Four blocks down the road, the car turned right into an alley. The detective stopped briefly, not wanting to be spotted. After about a minute, he drove slowly up the road. When he reached the alley where the car had turned, he looked. The car was gone. He turned into the alley in an effort to find the car again. After he passed through the alley, 6th Street connected with the alley in both directions. He stopped and looked both east and west down 6th Street. He didn't see any cars in either direction. The car had disappeared. For the next hour, the detective drove the streets in the area hoping to find the Taurus. He didn't find it.

***

Kevin Collins had been lucky. He was suspicious of the car that appeared to be following him. When he turned north on 5th Street, he spotted the headlights of the car about a hundred feet behind him. When the car turned off its headlights, he was certain he was being followed. He had been expecting this to happen. His brother was the blame.

He's made too many mistakes, and because of them, the police suspect him, Kevin thought.

He blamed Dennis for nearly getting him caught. He cared for his brother, but not as much as he cared for his addiction, his need to kill, his need to continue his work on the projects. If he had to sacrifice his brother to continue his work, he would. Dennis was weak—he had always been weak. Kevin had always known that at some point, he would need to do something about him. It appeared that now was that time.

He had a plan, but it would wait for a day or two. Now he had a body in the car, a fresh project. He pulled into the garage, wrapped the body in a tarp, and dragged it to the rear of the house, to the back door just off the kitchen. He opened it, turned on the light, and carried the body down the basement stairs and into the room with the cages. Five of the eight cages were empty now. He put his latest victim in the cage next to Rachel.

Rachel was his brother's favorite. He had developed a bond with her. Kevin had known there would come a time for Rachel to join the others as a finished project in the locked room, but there was no rush. There was no need to upset Dennis until it was absolutely necessary. He had intended for Rachel to be the last occupant of the cages to go to his workbench.

But for now, the people in the cages would need to wait. His projects needed to be put on hold. If he was going to be able to continue his work, something would need to be done now. Kevin needed to be beyond suspicion. He would need to sacrifice his brother. The police were onto Dennis. Soon they would get a search warrant and discover the basement. Kevin needed to act now.

The next afternoon, Kevin drove to the police department. He walked inside and went to the policeman at the front desk.

"May I speak to Detective Baczenas, please?"

"What's your name and what does this concern?" the policeman asked, barely lifting his head.

"My name is Kevin Collins, and I want to report several murders."

The policeman began to chuckle, thinking someone was playing a joke on him, but when he looked up at the young man in front of him, he could tell by the look on his face that this was no joke. He picked up the phone and dialed the detective's extension.

"Will, there is somebody here to see you. He says his name is Kevin Collis, and he has information about several murders."

The policeman hung up the phone and motioned for Kevin to step inside. He walked him back to Detective Baczenas's office and knocked on the door.

"Come in," the detective said.

For the next hour, Kevin talked about crimes he suspected his brother had committed. He talked about how his brother got started killing birds and small animals, then progressing to cats and dogs.

The detective had come to the house twice before. Once when an elderly neighbor, Mary Lou Brown, disappeared, and once after the disappearance of Barbara Johnson. Both times he talked to Dennis. Neither time did he see or speak to Kevin Collins. He wasn't even aware that Dennis had a brother for a long time.

He was the black sheep of the family, leaving home at an early age, the detective remembered

Those two disappearances remained open cases. Neither woman was ever seen again. Detective Baczenas was confident they had been murdered, but no body was found and there was no evidence of foul play.

It was Kevin that confirmed the detective's suspicions about the two cases.

"I'm pretty sure, Detective, that my brother murdered an elderly neighbor and her dog about ten years ago. I also think he murdered a woman at Kelly's bar, a stripper, I believe."

"What makes you think that, Mr. Collins?"

"My brother has had blackouts ever since our father died. He had one of those blackouts the day a neighbor disappeared, and another one the night a woman disappeared from Kelly's. He told me about the blackouts after the police came to question him. He was afraid he had done something bad to them while he was blacked out. Detective, my brother is very sick. I think he has killed several times."

"What makes you think that, Mr. Collins?"

"He told me about nightmares he has had. They seemed so vivid to him. In each one, he kills someone. He told me about a woman that was being attacked in the parking lot of Kelly's. He said he killed her attacker in his dream. He told me about a group of men that he attacked at another bar. He came to their rescue and shot one of the attackers."

"Okay, but if he did kill before, where are the bodies?"

"I think they are in that house, Detective."

"Have you ever seen one of the bodies, Mr. Collins?"

"No. But that doesn't mean they aren't there. Dennis keeps several rooms locked. He doesn't let me go into those rooms. I know he is trying to hide something."

Detective Baczenas called in a stenographer to take

down his statement. Then he had another person type it up for Kevin to sign. With the statement in hand, he went to a judge to get a search warrant for Dennis's house and car. As soon as he got the search warrant, the detective got in his car and headed to Dennis's house. He called Detective Moffit on the way.

"Dan, we have the search warrant. Get the team and meet me at his house. I'm heading there now."

CHAPTER 14
MOTHER'S DIARY

The pain at the back of his head was tremendous. The fall down the stairs had knocked him out for a few seconds. When he awoke, he was dazed. He tried to focus his eyes., tried to access what had happened. He reached for his gun, but it wasn't on him.

It must have fallen out when I fell, he thought.

It was completely dark in the basement. He staggered to his feet and reached around, hoping to find his gun. He moved in small circles around him, taking tiny steps, hoping to find his gun with one of those steps. That's when he felt the string touching the top of his head. He reached up and pulled it. The light flickered twice and turned on. The bulb was dim and only illuminated a small area near the stairs. He looked up the stairs hoping to get of glimpse of the person that had hit him, but no one was there. The door leading upstairs was closed.

Did I black out? he wondered.

He looked to the floor all around him, looking for the gun. It wasn't visible. The rain was pounding on the basement windows. He could hear it collide with the glass, but he could not see the windows.

They must be covered, he thought.

The light from the dim bulb didn't extend all the way to the wall. But it did expose three shelves containing birds and small animals.

What the hell? he thought.

Then a bolt of lightning illuminated the area closest to the windows. He saw the dark curtains covering the windows, and he saw the shadow. It streaked past the windows to the back of the basement.

Someone is down here, he said to himself.

The detective wasn't alone. He couldn't make out the shadowy figure, but he knew someone was there.

"Dennis, is that you?" he yelled.

He looked around one more time for his gun. It wasn't there. He moved quickly toward the wall where the light had come through the window. When he reached the first window, he opened the curtain. The rain and the fog outside dulled the streetlights, but some light did come through the window. He moved to the other two windows and opened the curtains that had been covering them. That provided a little more light, enough light to see the ominous creatures that lined one side of the wall. They were organized in rows, on shelves stacked from the floor of the basement to the ceiling, hundreds of them it looked like.

As he moved farther into the basement, he saw a door against the far wall. He approached it slowly, carefully, cognizant of his surroundings so not to be surprised from behind. He turned the knob on the door. It was not locked.

"Help, please help," he heard someone say.

"Police," he yelled. "If you are in here, come out with your hands up."

"He's not here. Please, help us," he heard a woman's voice say.

The room was completely dark. "Where's a light? Do you know where a light is?" he asked

"There's a chair just ahead of you. There is a light switch directly behind the chair on the wall," the person said.

He moved farther into the room until he bumped into the chair. He reached for the wall, located the light switch, and turned it on.

"Oh shit," he yelled when he saw the cages, eight of them lined up against the wall just across from him.

"Please, let us out of here," the woman yelled.

Detective Baczenas went to the cage where the woman was and opened it. He helped her out and pulled her to her feet. She was crying. She put her arms around him and held him tight.

"Thank you, thank you," she said. "Please get us out of here."

"What is your name?" the detective asked.

"Rachel," she said, fighting back the tears.

He opened the other cages and helped the other victims out. They were all asleep—heavily medicated, he assumed. One by one, he dragged three more victims from the cages, all women. They didn't wake up. He began shaking each, trying to wake them. After removing the last victim from her cage, he heard the door to the room shut and the lock being engaged. The detective rushed to the door, but it was too late. He was locked inside.

He kicked at the door. It wouldn't budge. Then the odor of gasoline crept into the room. He tried desperately to pry open the door. Suddenly a light penetrated from underneath the door frame. He heard a crackling sound. Then he smelled smoke. The basement was on fire.

***

Three police cars, lights flashing, sirens on, pulled up the driveway. Flames could be seen shooting from the basement windows. Smoke was billowing out of the house. Detective Moffit alerted the fire department from a block away after seeing the flames.

The detective and four officers went into the house through the front door. Smoke was dense on the first floor. They struggled through the smoke to get to the basement door.

"The door is warm," Detective Moffit said. "Everybody get back while I open it."

Smoke was pouring from the bottom of the door. Fire trucks could be heard coming down the road.

Detective Moffit opened the door quickly, jumping away as he did in case of a backdraft. There wasn't one, but the smoke was dense. Flames could be seen just to the right of the base of the stairs.

"Will, are you down there?" he hollered. There was no response.

He looked around the kitchen and spotted a dish towel. He grabbed it and dampened it in the sink. Then he put it on his head, covering much of his face.

"Go outside and wait for the firemen. Direct them down to the basement. I'm going down," he said.

The detective took a deep breath and ran down the stairs toward the flames. Fire trucks arrived at the house three minutes later. A pumper truck poured water into the main floor. Firefighters broke out the three basement windows. The oxygen from the outside fed the fire and flames shot out the broken windows. Hoses pumped massive amounts of water through the windows into the basement.

Six firefighters worked their way through the main floor to the basement door and down the stairs. The fire had burned through several of the bottom steps, disintegrating two of the steps and causing several others to buckle. Water gushing through their hoses paved the way for the firefighters to enter the basement.

"Over here," they heard a voice say.

They worked their way to the far end of the basement. Detective Moffit was lying on the floor, gasping for breath.

"Hold on, we'll get you out of here," the lead fireman said.

"There are people trapped behind this door," Detective Moffit said.

Two of the firefighters grabbed the detective and carried him out of the basement. Another firefighter used an axe to break through the door. Inside they found five people lying on the floor, two gasping for air, the other three unconscious.

Ambulances were waiting outside to take away the victims.

Smoke inhalation cost the lives of three of the victims.

Detective Baczenas, Rachel, and Detective Moffit survived.
***

Rachel's parents were at her side when she woke up in the hospital. She had thought about them often while she was in that cage. She wanted so badly to tell them how sorry she was for running away, for being so defiant, for being such a difficult child. But she never thought that she would see them again. Now her prayers had come true. Now she could start her life over again. Now she could right some of her wrongs.

"I love you, Mom and Dad. I'm so sorry for everything I've done. Can you please forgive me?"

Her mother, tears flowing down her face, put her arms around her daughter. "Honey, we never stopped loving you. We never stopped praying that you would come back to us. As soon as you're well, we'll go back home."

Her dad grabbed her hand, pulled it to his face, and kissed it. He was crying too. "We can't wait to have you home, Rachel. We've missed you so much."
***

A day after being checked in to the hospital, Detective Baczenas and Detective Moffit were back at their desks.

Dennis Collins had not been found in the house—he had escaped before the other police arrived. The fire in the basement destroyed most of what was in the main part of the basement, where the fire was started and where it was most intense.

The hidden room sustained smoke damage, but the fire did not penetrate its walls. The finished projects in the room remained undamaged. Detective Baczenas's team spent days identifying the victims in that room. With each victim identification, it became obvious they were dealing with a serial killer. The two victims of the vigilante were in that room. Mary Brown, Barbara Johnson, and Marsha Collins were in that room, also. All had been well-preserved, looking in death just like they'd looked in life. Each was dressed like they were attending a party. Disappearances dating back for over ten years were solved because of the discoveries in that room.

The body in the bed, embalmed to a near mummified state, was identified as Jane Collins, the mother. It was impossible to determine how long she had been dead, or the cause of her death. She was dressed in party clothes like the others, but her clothes were new. Receipts found indicated they were purchased only a week before her body was found.

A search was underway for Dennis Collins. He had disappeared after starting the fire. His car was found in the garage of the house. He did not escape in it.

Seventeen victims of Dennis Collins were discovered in the basement. He was the most prolific serial killer in Kansas City history.

He disappeared the night of the fire without a trace. His bank account, the bank account he had set up in Kevin's name, and his mother's bank account, along with her safety deposit box, were all emptied the day before the fire. The credit cards that had been issued in Dennis and his mother's name were never used after that night.

The airport, train station, and bus depots were all checked the days following the fire. There were no records of him using those modes of transportation. His picture was shown on all major news networks and in most major newspapers. Countless tips were investigated. Hundreds of people called a hotline set up to encourage tips and information about Dennis. None of those leads panned out.

Kevin Collins had vanished, too.

Every inch of the house where Dennis lived and every inch of Kevin's house were searched, looking for evidence and clues.

Fingerprints and DNA were taken from both locations and from the car.

It was in their mother's bedroom, in a diary that was kept between the mattresses where she slept, that the story of Dennis and Kevin Collins was told.

Jane Collins had documented everything that happened in that house for the last twenty-years in that diary.

July, 1985:
I'm pregnant, she wrote. *I just came from the doctor, and he gave me the good news. Ron is so excited. We're hoping for a boy.*

September, 1985:
I had a follow-up visit with the doctor. He found two heartbeats. He thinks they are both boys. We're going to name them Kevin and Dennis. Ron didn't take the news well. He's worried about money.

January, 1986:
Something is wrong. I was bleeding a lot today. I've been feeling ill for some time. Somedays I can barely get out of bed. I went to the doctor. He ran tests. I should have the results tomorrow.

Next day:

I went to the doctor today. The test results came back. My umbilocal cord is wrapped around one of my babies. His breathing has been labored. The doctor wants to perform a "C" section and remove the boys as soon as possible.

Three days later:
Kevin died today, three hours after he was born. I am heartbroken. At least God has blessed us with one healthy boy, Dennis.

Five days later:
We buried Kevin today. The funeral home provided us a child's casket and a funeral service. It was a private ceremony, just family. We buried Kevin at Mount Grace next to a tall, oak tree just overlooking a pond. It looked very peaceful. Ron seems to be doing fine. He's always been strong. But I don't know how I'm going to go on. I think about Kevin constantly. I can't stop crying.

June, 1986:
Ron has become distant. He is drunk more now. We don't talk much anymore. I think he is depressed, and blames me. He says I am the one that has become distant. He says I don't touch him or hold him like I used to. I know he is right, but it's not all my fault. He doesn't seem to try anymore either. I think the loss of Kevin is bothering both of us. But he thinks it's just me. He says he is fine.

July, 1986:
I can't stop thinking about Kevin. Ron won't even mention his name, and he screams at me if I do. I find myself calling Dennis by Kevin's name. I want Dennis to know about his brother. I don't want Kevin to be forgotten. Today I bought a boy doll. He has brown

hair and blue eyes. I told Dennis it was our secret. He could keep him in bed with him, but not to let his father find him. I told him the doll's name was Kevin. Dennis is too young to understand what happened to his brother, but someday I'll tell him.

February, 1988:
I told Dennis about his brother today. I think he understood, at least as well as any two-year old could. I told him the doll was like his older brother. He would be there for him at night, when he felt alone and scared, or when he just needed someone to talk to. God knows he won't get that from his father. Ron hardly says a word to him. He doesn't seem to care about Dennis at all. He just sits by that damn television set and drinks. Well, at least I've got Dennis.

June, 1988:
I hear Dennis in his room talking to the doll. I told Dennis to keep his voice down so his father doesn't hear him. When I went shopping the other day to buy him clothes, he asked me to buy some for Kevin. He even picked them out. It was so cute. I had to hide them in his room in case Ron came in. There is little chance of that though. He hasn't come in Dennis's room in months.

November, 1988:
Ron lost his job today. He is really depressed.

December, 1988:
Christmas is almost here. Ron is still unemployed. I'm not sure if we are going to be able to afford a present for Dennis. Ron seems to have given up on looking for a job until after the holidays. He's drinking more than I've ever seen him. If I try to talk to him about

it, he becomes angry.

Christmas Eve, 1988:
Ron hit me last night. I asked him if we could buy Dennis a small Christmas present. He became angry and slapped me. I'm not sure he even realized what he had done. He was so drunk. It hurt a lot last night, but my face is better now. There's a large red mark where he hit me across the cheek, but I covered it with make-up. Nobody can tell. I made Dennis a bed for Kevin today. It's not much and he won't be able to let his father see it, but I think he'll like it. I made it from a large shoe box I had in the attic. I cut the sides to make it look like a sleigh bed and I colored it blue, his favorite color. I'll give it to him tonight and tell him it's from Santa.

March, 1989:
Ron finally got a job today. It's at a Ford Plant on the north side of town. He'll be working the graveyard shift...a true blessing from God for me and Dennis. He won't be able to drink at night like he has been. I pray the beatings will stop now. Maybe now I can get a good night's sleep. Maybe now, Dennis will stop wetting the bed. Ever since the arguments intensified, Dennis seems to have withdrawn. I hear him talking to Kevin a lot more, but he rarely comes out of the bedroom and he doesn't talk to others. I've been worried about him, but with his dad gone at night, maybe everything will return to normal.

April, 1998:
Ron was laid off today. Business had slowed and the plant cut out the third shift. He received some severance, enough to get us by for a few months.

May, 1998:

Ron is drinking heavily again. He passed out in his chair last night. I tried to wake him and he swung at me. He missed, thank God, but I decided to let him sleep in the chair. He was still passed out this morning when Dennis left for school. He's so angry at night that I'm afraid to say anything to him. Dennis goes to his room as soon as he gets home from school. He's afraid of his father. I hear him talking to Kevin all the time now. He even made him a small new bed from a discarded child's bed he found. He placed it next to him on the floor between the wall and his bed, out of sight from his father if he should open the bedroom door. His bed-wetting started up again just recently. I think the arguing might have caused it to start again.

July, 1998:

Ron has become so angry. I'm afraid of him. Lately he has been beating me a lot. The violence has upset Dennis. I can hear him crying in his room. Ron hears him too. It just makes him more angry. I try to deflect that anger. I don't fight him when he beats me. But sometimes I'm not enough to alleviate his violence. Sometimes he goes after Dennis. I know I need to do something, but I don't know what. I've tried to leave him, but I always go back. I love him. I don't know why, but I do.

September, 1998:

I decided what I need to do about Ron. I had some money saved and took out a life insurance policy on him.

December, 1998:

I thought about poisoning Ron's drink tonight. I read that anti-

freeze was odorless and very effective. I filled his glass halfway full, poured a few ounces of anti-freeze, and mixed it. I started to bring it to him, but I stopped. I just couldn't do it. So, I poured the drink out and took the anti-freeze back to the garage.

One week later:

I went into the bedroom to talk to Dennis tonight. He was acting strangely. He was talking differently, faster. He seemed more agitated. I thought he was on drugs. Then he told me to stop calling him Dennis. He said his name was Kevin. I told him that wasn't true. Kevin was dead. I told him to never call himself Kevin again. We had a terrible argument. I'm worried about him.

January, 1999:

Ron is dead. We had a terrible fight last night. He beat me. I fell to the ground, bumping my head. I guess I passed out for a short while. When I woke up, I heard Ron in Dennis's room. They were screaming at each other. But it wasn't Dennis's voice. Dennis would never fight back. He would never curse at his father. He would never have the courage to threaten him. Whoever was in that room wasn't Dennis. Then I saw Dennis running out of the room toward the kitchen. Ron chased after him. He was terribly drunk, losing his balance several times, falling once. I followed him into the kitchen. He never noticed that I was behind him. The door to the basement was open. Ron yelled down for Dennis to come out. When he didn't, Ron started down the stairs. That's when I finally got the courage to do what needed to be done. I pushed him.

February, 1999:

I can't stop thinking about Ron. I feel so much guilt for what I did. I haven't been able to go into the basement. Every time I open the door,

I have flashbacks of him falling down those stairs. He had started a new hobby, taxidermy. The chemicals down in the basement give off a terrible odor every time that door is opened. Dennis has been going downstairs to secure and organize them.

March, 1999:
Life is getting better. I'm spending more time with Dennis. He's talking more. He seems to be coming out of his shell. I don't hear him talking to Kevin anymore, although I know his bed is still there next to Dennis. He seems happier than I've ever seen him. He's not spending as much time in his room. I think he enjoys spending time with me. I know I enjoy spending time with him. But I can't stop feeling lonely. I miss Ron. I need someone else in my life.

May, 1999: *started dating again. His name is Tom. He's moving in with me tomorrow. Dennis hasn't met him yet. I haven't even told him about Tom, but I think they'll get along fine.*

October, 1999:
Tom is dead. I am heartbroken. He had a heart attack last night. I don't know if I can ever love another man.

May, 2001:
I've fallen in love again. His name is Earl Chase. He's a lot older than me, but he is a wonderful, caring man.

July, 2001:
Earl asked me to marry him tonight. I said yes! I haven't told Dennis yet, but I think he likes Earl. I'm so happy.

December, 2001:

This is the saddest day of my life. Earl is gone. He disappeared, just two weeks before our wedding. I woke up yesterday. His clothes were gone. His car was gone. I tried calling him, but the call went unanswered. I keep hoping he'll come back. We had an argument last night, but I can't imagine that causing him to leave. He didn't even leave a note. I don't know what to do or who else to call.

Two weeks later:

Today was supposed to be our wedding day. There is still no sign of Earl. He doesn't answer my calls. I've gone to the bar where we met. No one has seen or heard from him. I'm so depressed I can barely get out of bed. Dennis brings me food and sits and watches television with me. I know he loves me and wants me to get better, but I just can't seem to get going. I can't stop thinking about Earl.

May, 2002:

I went to the doctor today. It was everything I could do to get out of bed and leave the house. Dennis went with me. The doctor prescribed something to help with depression, and also anxiety medication to help me relax at night. The sleeping pills just aren't enough now. Nights are the worst. Dennis has been absolutely wonderful.

November, 2002:

I don't want to live. I tried cutting my wrists, but Dennis found me in the bathroom. The wounds weren't very deep. He bandaged them up. I don't know if I've got the courage to take my own life.

April, 2003:

I fell last night. I didn't fracture anything, but my back is in terrible pain.

August, 2003:
The doctor prescribed OxyContin for my back pain. It seems to be working, although I'm tired all the time. I haven't been out of the bed except to go to the doctor for several weeks.

July, 2003:
I don't know what I'd do without Dennis. He takes such good care of me. I feel guilty. He should be dating, or with friends. Instead he spends all of his free time taking care of me. I can't seem to get out of bed anymore. My back pain is tremendous. The pills aren't working like they used too.

October, 2003:
Dennis found a clinic downtown where he can get a higher dosage of the pain medication. I'm feeling better now, but I'm sleeping most of the day. I'm also having some strange dreams. At night, I hear voices coming from the basement. Sometimes I hear screams. Dennis says it is a side effect of the medication I'm taking.

April, 2004:
I woke up in the middle of the night. At, least I thought I woke up. It could have been a nightmare. Dennis was standing over me looking down at me, quiet, just watching. He had an odd expression on his face. He was holding a knife. I was startled. I asked him what he was doing. He told me that he was considering killing me. I knew from the voice that it wasn't Dennis standing over me. It was Kevin.

May, 2005:

I keep having that reoccurring nightmare. It is always the same, Kevin standing over me in the middle of the night, always with a disturbing look on his face and a slight smile. He threatens to kill me soon. I'm afraid of him. I've told Dennis about him, but he tells me not to worry. Kevin no longer stays in the house. He tells me it must be a nightmare, a side effect of my medication.

February, 2006:
The noises in the basement are getting louder. I hear screams almost every night. Dennis is working at the funeral home now. He isn't around as much as he used to be. I'm afraid. I can't get out of bed, and I have no way to protect myself.

June, 2007:
Kevin was in my room last night. He told me that Dennis didn't need me anymore. He only needed Kevin. He told me the end was near, that he would kill me soon. After he left, I tried calling the police. The phone was dead.

That turned out to be the last entry in Jane's diary.

CHAPTER 15
THE SEARCH FOR DENNIS

The FBI got involved in the hunt for Dennis. They had experience bringing serial killers to justice. They had resources that were vastly superior to those of the Kansas City police force.

A team of psychologists and criminal profilers studied his past behavior and habits to try to determine what motivated his actions. He was like no person with multiple personalities that they had studied before. Dennis had created an entirely separate life. He had a social security number in Kevin's name, a driver's license in his name, and he had credit cards, bank accounts, and a diploma from mortuary school in Kevin's name. Kevin paid taxes.

It was determined that Dennis used the birth certificate of Kevin to create the documentation for an entirely separate life. That took calculation. It took planning. It took someone that wanted desperately to be Kevin, to have a completely separate life. Kevin married.   His stepdaughters were interviewed. They had no idea that their stepfather was anyone other than Kevin. From all accounts, his wife had no idea either.

He had even altered his looks. That was a mystery that even the FBI profilers had no explanation for. No one recognized that Dennis and Kevin were the same person. They looked similar, but not the same. They looked like brothers. Their mannerisms were unique. Their voices were unique. They styled their hair differently and they walked and talked differently.

Hundreds of tips came in to the police hotline, but none proved helpful. It was as if he completely disappeared. The search for Dennis Collins eventually became a cold case, an unsolved case, that would haunt the unsolved case files of the Kansas City Police Department for years to come.

It became the case that Detective Baczenas would never forget, the most prolific killer he had ever come across, and the one suspect he was never able to bring to justice. Dennis Collins haunted his nightmares. Even after he retired ten years later, he continued to search for him.

Most people assumed Dennis Collins was dead. Will Baczenas was not one of those people. He was certain he was alive, and still killing people. He was equally certain that someday, he would find him.

The case of Dennis Collins possessed him. When he was retired, he tried to relax, to enjoy life. Police work had cost him three marriages and one heart attack. He had been a workaholic. He was driven. Marriage and family took a back seat to his work. He had never learned to slow down, to smell the roses.

His heart attack nearly killed him, and made him reflect on his life, appreciate things a little more. It was the driving force in his decision to retire.

He began going to church—he had not been since he was a small boy. He tired of it quickly. Church and God had done little for the victims of violence he had known over the years. Will was wrong to think they would give him peace.

He took up fishing. That lasted about a week. He didn't have the patience for it.

So, he tried golf. He found the nineteenth hole to be the only one he enjoyed.

Will knew retirement was a mistake after two weeks. He needed to be active. He needed to find the one criminal that had gotten away from him.

There will be plenty of time to rest when I'm dead, he told himself.

Will began going to the library, reading newspapers and crime articles from as many major markets as he could find.

There would be news of disappearances, he thought.

He was convinced that Dennis Collins had changed his identity and was killing again. He was certain he had selected a large market. It provided a larger hunting ground, and was easier for him to blend in.

Every day, he spent hours scrolling through news articles searching for disappearances, some pattern of unsolved crimes. It took nearly a year, but Will's diligence paid off. He noticed a pattern of disappearances from the Chicago market. He plotted the locations of the crimes and noticed that most happened in a specific section of North Chicago.

The victims had similarities too. Many were prostitutes. Some were homeless. Some disappeared just after leaving bars. They were similar to many of the victims found in Dennis's basement.

Will became convinced that Dennis was alive and living in the Chicago market. He passed his theory to a contact he had with the FBI, but he heard nothing back.

He was not the type of person to wait for someone else to enter the chase. He presented the FBI with what he had discovered because that was what he was supposed to do. That certainly didn't mean he would stop working the case.

There was something that had always bothered him about Dennis Collins's efforts to begin a separate life way back when he was a teenager.

He must have planned it for something, Will thought. *Those weren't the actions of someone with multiple personalities. Those were the actions of someone that was clever and calculating, not someone that was struggling with their identity.*

Dennis had taken his brother's birth certificate and used it to get a social security number. He used it to get a driver's license, open bank and savings accounts, buy a house, and get a job, all using Kevin Collins's identity.

Even the FBI psychiatrists and profilers agreed that was highly unusual from someone suffering with multiple personalities. People suffering with that illness almost always took on other personalities gradually, over an extended amount of time. The identity they were born with remained dominant, gradually succumbing to their other personalities. Many times, they were not even cognizant of their other personality for a long time.

Since Dennis began working on a separate identity at such a young age, not only was he cognizant of Kevin Collins's existence, but he must have already succumbed to it being his dominant personality, Will speculated. *Is it possible that he never had a split personality, that he was using that illness as an excuse for his actions?* Will wondered.

Suddenly, Will had an epiphany.

Why didn't it dawn on me sooner? he thought. *It was so obvious.*

Dennis Collins had planned that last day. He had planned his escape. He knew what was going to happen in that basement long before it did. Will Baczenas had been a pawn. Dennis had played him.

But maybe, just maybe, Will thought, *he went back to his similar success to aid in his escape.*

He went through his old case files and looked up the names and personal information about each of Dennis Collins's victims. Then he researched property owned recently and, also previously, by each of the victims. There were thousands of properties owned by various people with those names throughout the country, but Will was only interested in the properties owned in or near Chicago. There were three of them. He mapped the location and purchase dates of each.

A huge smile came over his face. Without a doubt, Will knew where Dennis Collins was living.

***

It was February. Chicago had experienced bitter cold for nearly a week. Temperatures dipped below zero. Wind chills were twenty below. Lake Geneva was even colder. There was over a foot of snow on the ground. Much of the lake was frozen.

Earl Chase owned a small coffee shop on Main Street. He'd bought it ten years earlier. Lake Geneva, Wisconsin was a small, picturesque resort community in Southeast Wisconsin, about eighty miles north of Chicago. The coffee shop was busy during tourist season, but for seven months out of the year, the only customers that came in were locals. The community was used to transient people. Businesses came and went. Strangers were commonplace, and during the summer, everyone blended in. The locals kept to themselves. They worked hard during the summer months and used the off-season to relax. Lake Geneva suited Earl Chase just fine.

The coffee shop was closed by the time Will arrived. The wind and blowing snow had slowed him, and it was nearly suppertime when he pulled into town. He ate at a diner just down the street from the coffee shop. He used that opportunity to get directions to the farmhouse where Earl lived.

The farmhouse was located on a desolate piece of land five miles outside of town. Rural backroads blanketed in snow were the only way to get there. It was freezing cold outside. Wind was blowing the snow, making visibility difficult. It was dark by the time he pulled onto the dirt road that led to the farmhouse. When he reached the mailbox at the bottom of a hill about five-hundred-feet from the house, he stopped the car, turned off the engine, and walked the remainder of the way. He wanted his arrival to be a surprise. Will checked the mailbox. It contained no mail, but a name was on the box, "Chase."

The gravel driveway leading up to the house was

covered in snow, eight inches deep. Two pairs of tire tracks were the only areas the snow had been disturbed. The sky was dark, the moon not visible behind the clouds. Blowing snow flew into Will's face and clouded his vision.

Will walked slowly, defiantly up that driveway. The farmhouse was old, weathered, and in bad need of a coat of paint. It sat at the top of a hill overlooking the countryside. The house was two-stories with a large wooden front porch. There were no porch lights, and no lights on the main or second floor. There was a dim light coming from the side of the house near the ground, a basement light.

He should have been nervous—he'd expected to be. But he wasn't. He had been waiting for this day for a long, long time.

He stepped onto the stairs leading up to the porch. They were wooden and old and squeaked and bowed with every step. The porch made the same noise, even louder.

If he is upstairs, the noisy porch will have alerted him, he thought.

When he got to the front door, Will pulled out a gun he had in a shoulder harness. It was the same type of gun he'd brought with him ten years earlier, the same type he'd lost when he fell down the basement stairs.

He turned the knob on the front door. It was unlocked, just like it had been ten years earlier. Will pulled out a flashlight from his coat. There was a light switch on the wall just to the right of the front door, but he chose not to use it. He didn't want to alert Dennis.

He moved the flashlight from side-to-side, surveying the room. The walls were bare. The room he entered from the front door was a good size, and a large stone fireplace occupied most of one wall. There were only three pieces of furniture in the room—a reclining chair, a small coffee table, and a television set. Each itemed looked old and used, something one would expect to see thrown out as garbage.

As Will got closer to the chair, he noticed something just barely sticking out from the top of the headrest. It looked like strands of hair.

Is somebody or something sitting in the chair? he wondered.

The back of the chair was in front of him. He couldn't make out the object sitting in the chair. Gun raised and flashlight pointed directly at the back of the recliner, he touched the armrest and swiveled the chair around.

Shivers ran down his back. He nearly dropped the flashlight. Sitting in the chair was a male doll, nearly life size, certainly over five-feet tall and very lifelike. It had graying hair. It was dressed in a blue, pinstriped suit, white shirt, and red tie, with cufflinks attached to the tailored sleeves bearing the initials DC. The doll was wearing navy blue dress socks and black dress shoes, recently shined.

What the hell? Will said to himself. He felt chills running through his body.

The detective wanted to get out of the house, but he couldn't. He had come too far and waited too long for this moment. So, he continued, but not through the rest of the house. He had done that before, and it hadn't ended well.

Will knew where Dennis would be—he was in the basement. If Will was to have any element of surprise, he would need to go there now. He moved carefully and quietly to the door off the kitchen that he thought was most likely the basement door. The detective moved the flashlight from side-to-side to all areas around the door. He had been fooled before and it almost cost him his life. Will would be certain this time that no one was lurking around the corner, waiting to push him down the stairs again.

Certain that no one was hiding nearby, Will opened the basement door, slightly at first, then all the way. The area below the main floor was more like a large cellar than a basement. The walls were made of brick, the floor, at least the area at the bottom of the stairs, was dirt. There was a light on somewhere in the basement. The edges of it extended to the bottom two steps. He closed the basement door behind him and started down the wood steps. Only eight steps to the basement. The ceiling, no more than six feet tall, forced Will to duck to fit his 6'5" frame inside.

The cellar was cold and damp. There didn't appear to be a heat source. The light was coming from another room at the far end of the cellar. The door was partially open and the light was bright. It came from the ceiling and illuminated most of the cellar.

The cellar was mostly empty. A shelf on one side of the room contained canned goods. Another shelf contained household supplies, but there was nothing out of the ordinary.

The room straight ahead where the light was coming from became his focal point. Twenty-seven steps. His heart pounding harder with each step he took, twenty-seven steps and he was at the door. Inside the room the floors were concrete, the walls were plastered, the ceiling was eight-feet high and long, and a bright fluorescent light fixture hung from the ceiling. The room inside was small, about the size of a bedroom. It smelled of antiseptic, similar to the smell inside a hospital. On one side of the room was a workbench, clean and uncluttered. Tools hung above the bench, typical tools one would expect to see above a workbench.

At the back of the room was a long, narrow hallway, maybe three feet wide. There was no lighting in that area, and the hallway extended beyond the area illuminated by the lights in the room he was standing. There was complete darkness down the hall.

The detective walked down the hallway, slowly, carefully, stopping every few seconds to listen for any sound. It was eerily quiet. Thirty feet down the narrow hallway, Will reached the edge of the light. Everything beyond was dark. He lifted his flashlight and continued. Fifteen more feet and he reached a second door, this one metal. Will reached for the handle and turned it. It was unlocked. He pulled the door open.

The room was completely dark. He shined the flashlight inside, turning it from side-to-side, up and down. The narrow light captured something darting past it. He heard another door open and shut.

"Whoever is in here, I have a gun. Show yourself," Will yelled. He reached for a light switch. There was one, just to the right of the door. He flipped it on.

Inside were a dozen wire cages, about the size of large dog kennels. There were six bodies, bound and lying curled up in six of the cages. The others were empty. All the victims in the cages were alive, sleeping.

Will focused his attention on the door at the rear of the room. He moved to it and turned the handle. It was unlocked.

He opened it. The light was on. Dennis Collins was seated in a chair on the other side of the room.

"What took you so long to find me, Detective?" he said.

"I'm not a detective any more, Mr. Collins. I retired."

Dennis laughed. "Evidently not. What was the matter, couldn't you stop thinking of me?"

"You knew I'd never stop looking for you."

"I know, Detective. The question is, now that you've found me, what are you going to do with me?"

"Oh, I think you know the answer to that, Dennis."

"Well, before you do what you need to do, what do you think of my work?"

Dennis motioned to one side of the room. In glass cases that stretched from the floor to the ceiling were his newest finished projects, all women, all with similar looks, wearing similar clothes, looking like they were attending a party. Everyone resembled his mother.

"You're a very sick person, Dennis."

"Dennis died in that basement, ten years ago."

Will raised his gun toward Dennis.

"Go ahead and shoot, Detective. No one will blame you. You'll be doing me a favor."

"I'm not going to kill you, Mr. Collins. I'm going to take you in. Put your hands out in front of you," he said, reaching for a pair of handcuffs.

"I'm sorry, Detective. I can't let you do that."

Dennis stood, raising a gun that had been concealed.

"Put the gun down, Mr. Collins. You don't want it to end this way."

"Sorry, but I have no other options."

Two shots rang out. Both men fell to the ground.

Dennis Collins's gun went off slightly after the gun Will Baczenas held. His shot was slight skewed by the impact of the bullet hitting his chest.

The altered trajectory of the bullet penetrated Will's right shoulder. He was injured but not killed. Dennis Collins was not as lucky. Will was a very good shot.

-The End-

Alan Brown grew up in the suburbs of Kansas City and graduated from Shawnee Mission East High School in 1973 and Avila University in 1979. Now he lives in a suburb of St. Louis, MO with my wife and three daughters. He also has four sons that are grown and living outside the home. He enjoys writing about experiences he had growing up, examining the fantastical side, the dark side of a person's natural fears. All of his books are based on a reality in his life. He is a fan of Alfred Hitchcock. Like his stories, Alan Brown's will conclude with a twist, something he hope will take the reader by surprise.